Dec/14

D0767305

Also by Grace Dent

Fame and Fortune

Grace Dent

Hodder
Children's
Books

A division of Hachette Children's Books

A Catalogue record for this book is available from the British Library

ISBN-13: 978 0 340 97064 5

Typeset in New Baskerville by Avon DataSet Ltd,
Bidford-on-Avon, Warwickshire

Printed and bound by CPI Group (UK) Ltd, Croydon, CR0 4YY

The paper and board used in this paperback by Hodder Children's Books
are natural recyclable products made from wood grown in
sustainable forests. The manufacturing processes conform to the
environmental regulations of the country of origin.

Hodder Children's Books
A division of Hachette Children's Books
338 Euston Road, London NW1 3BH
An Hachette UK Company
www.hachette.co.uk

For Emily Thomas, who is well choong and bare jokes.

This diary belongs to:

Shiraz Bailey Wood

Address: 34, Thundersley Road,
            Goodmayes,
            Essex,
            BRAP 100

OCTOBER

MONDAY 3RD OCTOBER

10am – Thundersley Road, Goodmayes, Essex.

I'm not usually made up on being the centre of attention.

No, Shiraz Bailey Wood just don't understand all these wannabe celeb types always wanting to be in the spotlight with the whole world proper beholding their choongness saying, 'Wow, bruv, you're amaaaazing!'

That ain't me at all. I'm all about keeping it real.

But my birthday's a whole new story. I don't mind a bit of fuss on my birthday. Y'know, singing songs and pressies and all that? Like maybe one of them well lovely ASDA caterpillar cakes with Smarties eyes and chocolate butter fondant cream filling, the ones that make you feel well sick after two slices, but you still have three anyway, then have a vomit incident on a bouncy castle? And a birthday card from my nan, with a little girl on the front frolicking with a hoolahoop, what Nan buys from the hideous 1980s card shop at the end of a time tunnel, where nans always get birthday cards from. Oh and I LOVE that bit when you open your card and something flutters out with the Queen's face printed on it, and you take that down to Top Shop and exchange it for jeans or earrings or something you actually want! I like all that sort of birthday thing. And as far as Shiraz Bailey Wood birthdays go, this one ain't been so bad up to now.

'Happy Birthday To Yooooooou!' our Murphy sang to me this morning as I was eating my bowl of Aldi Brekkie Chocobangbangs and watching *Friends* on Channel 4.

'Happy Birthday to yooooooou!
You look like you've got cat AIDS!
And you smell like old poooooooo!
HAHAHAHAHAHHAHAHAHAH!!!!!
Happy Birthday Shizbiz!!!'

Murphy was well happy with his song, 'cos he was laughing his head off and then he grabbed my head and ruffled it till my scrunchie stood up like a pineapple. And he blew a farty raspberry sound on my forehead and shouted, 'HA MOONMASK MOONMASK MOOON MASK! OH MY GOD YOUR FOREHEAD IS LIKE THE MOON!'

'Murphy!' shouted Ritu, Murphy's Japanese girlfriend, giving him a well good dead arm. 'No say Shiraz got cat AIDS! It not nice to your sister! It not respectful! We been talk about respect Murphy? You be respect to people, you get respect back, innit?' says Ritu.

'It's OK, Ritu,' I said. 'I'm used to it.'

'Soz, Shizza,' Murph said, laughing to himself but looking a bit guilty, then passing me a box wrapped in shiny purple paper with a pink ribbon.

This is a good example of why my mother is letting

Ritu from Japan stay at our house 'on the sofa' in Essex when she should be in Osaka finishing her studies. Because Ritu is proper good at making Murph listen to reason. (I just wish she wouldn't 'reason with him' through my bedroom wall every night. OMG RITU IS NO WAY SLEEPING ON THE SOFA AND IT IS WELL RANK! I HAVE TO SLEEP WITH MY IPOD ON SHUFFLE TO BLOCK OUT THEIR WILD GRUNTS O' LOVE. BLEUGHGHGH!

Anyways, filthy lovegrunts aside, Murph and Ritu bought me a proper nice Ruby and Millie make-up box for my birthday! Beautiful it is too. Oh, and they got me some well expensive moisturiser cream from this posh makeup shop, SpaceNK. I would have been made up about it, but . . . when I looked closer it was for bloody eye wrinkles!! EYE WRINKLES???

'Sorry, Shiraz,' Ritu said. 'I tell Murphy to buy face moisturiser but he get mix up. It very good wrinkle cream, though!'

'Oh, oh . . . no worries, thank you!' I said, looking at the packet which had this well sad picture on the front of some woman who was proper ancient, about thirty-four years old or something, staring at herself in the mirror probably thinking something proper tragic like, 'Ooh it's Friday, best get meself down Marks and Spencer and buy some elasticated waist trousers and a nice broccoli quiche and come home and listen to me James Blunt CD 'cos I don't need to look bare choong no more what with me being almost dead, in fact the minging trousers will be something smart to cremate me in'.

OK, I'll be honest, the wrinkle cream made me feel sort of spooked out. I don't like getting older at all. It only seems like about six days ago I was in the bloody headmaster's office with Uma at Mayflower Academy, getting well nagged for that time Uma wrote MR BOMBLECLOT BUMS CATS on the detention room wall in twenty-centimetre high letters in neon pink Boots Number 7 nail varnish what she'd thieved. OH MY DAYZ we got well shouted at for that! Anyways, that wasn't six days ago, IT WAS SIX YEARS AGO, WHEN I WAS THIRTEEN! I want this getting older thing to stop now if that's all right, please. THANK YOU PLEASE BABY JESUS, ta.

Then, my big sister Cava-Sue wanders in looking all excited. Well as excited as an emo can possibly look 'cos even when Cava-Sue is looking well excited, like today on my birthday it's important that everyone remembers that she is an emo and she's wearing black on the outside of her body 'cos black represents how she is feeling in her cold, black, emo heart what has been so destroyed by decades of pain and disappointment, man.

Hahahah! Me and Murphy say this sort of stuff to Cava-Sue a lot and laugh our heads off but Cava-Sue doesn't laugh much back, in fact she says we are both well childish and totally emo-ist which is a HATE CRIME ACTUALLY. And then she goes upstars and puts on her new favourite CD, *Tsunami of Suffering* by Fire In The Petting Zoo.

We're only winding Cava-Sue up obviously. Cava-Sue ain't really miserable – well, not much, and especially not on birthdays. Cava-Sue loves birthdays more than the person having the birthday 'cos it gives her a chance to organise things and get her clipboard and list out and be bossy.

'Happy Birthday, Little Shiz!' she yelled at me this morning, pouncing on me and giving me a big hug. My face went in her freshly crimped hair and I nearly got a big Aldi Chocobangbang smudge on the shoulder of her Goodmayes Council Recycling Nazi uniform.

Serious, I'm well proud of Cava-Sue at the moment, 'cos she has just had a promotion at work, which means she is now a 'Junior Environmental Manager'! This means she don't only get to hassle folk about their recycling boxes and knock on their door and give them earache for not washing out their baked bean cans. No, NOW Cava-Sue gets to visit schools, too, and talk to kids about saving the environment. She is well enjoying that!

Our Cava-Sue has well been creating havoc and terror through Essex. Last week she got an entire class of eight-year-olds proper widdling their pants hysterical by showing them a photo of a three-eyed fish in Russia and telling them this was all their mothers' faults for poisoning the oceans with Daz liquid tablets!

Hahahhahah! Cava-Sue is well good with shock tactics,

innit? Sadly Miss Khan the headmistress weren't really feeling Cava-Sue's speech, and she sent a letter the next day saying my sister ain't allowed back in St Oswald's Primary School again any time this century. Still, there's loads of other schools my sister can visit. Cava-Sue reckons not everyone is 'narrow-minded and non-progressive'. Good on her.

'Right, Shiz,' Cava-Sue said to me this morning. 'You're getting mine and Lewis's present and card later at your special birthday tea! Now you've told Wesley Barrington Bains II that we're having a birthday tea haven't you? YOU DID REMEMBER??? He knows what time to come?'

'Yeah, 'course I have,' I said, really, really hoping I had. I always forget stuff like this. I am beginning to realise I am a rubbish girlfriend. When you're a full-time proper girlfriend you have to remember all sorts of things like this. It's like looking after two people, not one. I'm always messing up.

'Hey, I wonder what Wes is getting you for a pressie, Shizza? He's such a sweetheart,' Cava-Sue says to me looking all dopey. 'Hey, you might get another ginormous bear! Oh Shiraz, remember that bear. The one you could hardly get up the stairs. And remember when he did that thing with the blue Smarties? He saved up all the blue ones 'cos he knew they were your favourites!'

'Gnnngnngnn yeah,' I said, sort of laughing but

feeling well bad. See, my Wesley is well good at being a boyfriend. He don't mind remembering enough stuff for two. He loves it in fact.

'I can't wait to see what he shows up with today.' Cava-Sue laughed, starting to make some breakfast.

To be honest, I told Wes that what I'd really really like for my birthday, if he was going to spend money, was for him to help me towards buying my own laptop. I've got my eye on one in the sale down at PC World, I've been saving up all my wages from my new job for it. But if Wes helped me I could get it much sooner. I bloody love faffing about on the internet I do. Not just piddling about on Bebo and MSN and stuff, I love finding out about all sorts of stuff all over the world, places to travel to and things to see and all that. To be honest, and this is a secret I'm not letting anyone know, I'm really beginning to miss not learning anything any more. Like I was when I was doing my AS-Levels. Proper expanding my mind. I totally wish I'd gone back and spoken to Ms Bracket at Mayflower Sixth Form back in September, and asked her about doing the other half of my A-Levels. But I never got it together 'cos I'd just got back from Ibiza, and got back with Wes, and it just sort of never happened. The other half of the AS-Levels are meant to be well hard, though. And I'd need to give up my job and I'd be totally skint if I couldn't do my babysitting, and my babysitting is during the day when all my classes are! Agggggh! I feel like all that's slipping away from me now. A career and all that. That's why it would be good to have the laptop. I don't want to forget that there's a life outside of Goodmayes. I mentioned the laptop to Wesley but he didn't seem that keen. Dunno why. It's not like I mind when he plays *Grand Theft Auto* for six hours in a row some Sundays.

'Oh my life Cava-Sue, I hope he's not getting me another bear,' I said to her, sighing a bit.

Cava-Sue looked at my well serious face and giggled.

'Awwwww, little Shiz! Look at your face? Cheer up! 'Ere, which birthday is this again!?' she said, jamming two pieces of her special disgusting high fibre sunflower seed and squirrel bumchunk bread into the toaster.

'Nineteen,' I groaned.

'Nineteen!?' she squeaked back at me.

Nineteen bloody years old. That proper gives me the bumholeshudders that does.

Nineteen. That well sounds like someone boring and sensible.

OH MY DAYZ – hear me now – Shiraz Bailey Wood will never EVER be sensible END OF! I am the anti-sensible. Like, if I was sensible, would I have gone down Ilford McDonalds with my my best mate Carrie Draper last Saturday and bought Chicken McNugget Happy Meals so we could get the amazing free Disney Movie 'Parrot Fandango' toy trumpets? AND then got so well excited with the amazing free toy trumpets that we PARPED and HONKED the aformentioned amazing toy trumpets on the front seat of the bus home, until the bus driver had a proper shitfit and made us walk the last three stops back to Thundersley Road?! Hahahhahaha! The old git said it wasn't proper music! Hah! We were playing 'Smack That' by Akon if he'd been listening proper! It was well amazing choonage. Anyway, does that sound sensible to you?

And if I was sensible would I have gone round Kezia's house two weeks ago to cheer her up 'cos she's preggo and grumpy and spent the night making her laugh by calling up the local taxi firm, Call-Me-A-Cab and every time the bloke answered with 'Hello, call-me-a-cab', I started shouting, 'You're a cab! You're a cab! You're a cabbycabbycabCAB!' Then put the phone down and then called him ten more times until poor Kezia nearly popped her new baby out right there in front of the telly, four months early, from laughing! See, THAT IS NOT SENSIBLE! I am KRRRAZZY – with a capital K and extra 'r' and 'z's just to keep the 'madness' locked in.

And sensible nineteen-year-old people DEFINITELY DO NOT eat Aldi Brekkie Chocobangbangs what make your lips go purple and have so much refined sugar in them they give you swivelly eyes and a sweaty bum crevice. No, I think you'll find that nineteen-year-olds probably eat mueseli.

'What you thinking about, Shiraz? You look miles away,' Cava-Sue said to me this morning. I was staring out of the kitchen window watching our silly dog Penny rolling about on her back on the concrete with her paws in the air, proper loving the morning sun. She was probably rolling about on a dead mouse or something. She can be well rank our Penny, sometimes. Stupid bloody thing, I love her to death I do.

'Muesli,' I said to Cava-Sue. 'What's in that muesli stuff?'

'Muesli?' Cava-Sue said. 'Oooh, well, all sorts of slow release energy stuff. Locally sourced sustainable foods! Rolled oats, dried fruit . . .'

'Dog fangita, bum gravy . . .' snortled Murph, under his breath.

'Bum gravy? What that?' says Ritu. 'I no heard that food?'

'Berries, nuts,' says Cava Sue, ignoring them both. 'Much better than that choco-sugar crap you're eating there. Hey! I could get you some down Romford farmers' market? There's a woman down there called Spiderflower who's a white witch, right? Six toes she's got on one foot! Awful nice she is! She makes her own muesli in her bath!! She crushes the pecan nuts herself with her heels!'

'Nah, s'alright,' I said, feeling a bit chundersome. 'I'll stick with my Chocobangbangs.'

'OK, well I'm off to work now,' Cava-Sue chirped. 'How many babies you looking after today, aside from my Fin? Two?'

'Yeah,' I said, 'Kezia's mum is bringing Tiq for a few

hours and Colette is dropping off her little boy Rudi until three this afternoon.'

'Bloody hell,' said Murph, standing up and grabbing his rucksack. 'It's gonna be baby central here. I am definitely going to college.'

'I walk with you for fresh air,' said Ritu. 'It my day off from Mr Yolk today.' Then the pair disappeared off out of the door, holding hands and pinching each other's bums, and looking all well happy and loved-up.

'OK, Shiz,' Cava-Sue said, grabbing her handbag. 'Fin's just had his morning bottle and he's sitting in his cot playing with Macca Pacca. You're fine with everything aren't you?'

'Yeah, totally fine,' I said. 'Stop fretting.'

'And you'll be OK if he starts screaming? His ear's still a bit funny. It's a bit gooey. He's not over that cold thing he had.'

'He'll be fine. Just go to work, Cava-Sue!' I said.

We've been through this three times a week for the past five weeks.

'And what will you do if he suddenly gets a temperature or a rash!? Or he starts coughing again!?' Cava Sue said doing her weird, mental-mother, wide-eyed face.

'I'll just shove him in the under-the-stairs cupboard and tell folk the pikeys took him,' I said to her.

'You'll do what!!?!' said Cava-Sue.

'I'll call the medical centre and book an emergency appointment with Dr Gupta,' I said.

'Awwww, thanks, Shiz! You're a star, honest to God you are!' Cava-Sue laughed. 'I don't know how you're so calm with all these babies! You're a natural, you are! You'll be amazing when you have your own!! It's a gift Shiraz, honest. I dunno how you spend all day here with three of them. I'd go bloody full blown mental!'

'Yeah,' I said, sighing a bit. 'I rock, I know.'

After everyone had cleared off I stood there for a bit looking at myself in the mirror above the fire place, with my hoodie on over my pyjamas and those gold hoops on that my Wesley bought me as our getting-back-together-for ever after Ibiza gift.

'OH MY DAYZ!' I thought, 'I'm sure I look older and more boring than I did yesterday!!!'

This is how it begins, innit? First the boring face, then the elasticated trouser eye cream, then the box of sensible mutant toe-cheese muesli for breakfast. THIS AIN'T HAPPENING TO ME! I'VE GOT TO SORT THIS OUT!!

10.45pm – in my bedroom.

No one seems to have sussed yet that I've left my own party and went to bed. Not that it wasn't a good night, it was well funny having all the Woods and assorted hangers-on all in one room. I love 'em all to bits I do. I love the bones of them. It's just that I'm a bit knackered and my Wes brought his copy of *Guitar Hero III* round and it's all got a bit messy down there. My ears are proper ringing 'cos we've had the telly up at full volume blaring, 'cos Nan's husband Clement's hearing aid battery has gone flat. He reckons he can't hear *Enter Sandman* by Metallica unless he stands right next to the screen with the sound up at level ten!

Clement well loves playing to Metallica which is bare jokes 'cos he is eighty-three years old and only listens to *Gardener's Question Time* on Radio 4 usually. I've said to our Wes and Murph in private that I don't reckon a pensioner should be getting so over-excited, and if he carks it right there on Mother's good Littlewoods rug then it's THEIR RESPONSIBILITY, 'cos they encouraged him to play battle mode with them! Murph and Wes both just laugh at me and tell me to chill out and stop fretting.

Anyway, tonight was a typical Wood family affair full of laughing and chatting and joking and eating and arguing. And of course at least one situation where one of us was nearly in tears and another one of us was getting all het up with them and someone else was stepping in shouting, 'Oi! Come on? We've all had a drink! This is supposed to be a party!'

And there was the usual moment when Penny our dog had too many sausage rolls and started coughing up flecks of pastry and her snout had gone a bit green and my mother starts shouting, 'Oh my god! Penny is having a stroke! She's having a stroke! Call the vet!'

And Dad shouted, 'No she's not, she's just bloody ate herelf silly as usual, let her out for some fresh air!'

And as usual our Cava-Sue stood on the sofa and gave one of her speeches about 'taking stock of the year what's just past', which basically just meant reminding everyone in fine detail about the fact I gave up my A-Levels to go to London and worked as a Magic Elf in a Christmas grotto before going off to Ibiza and getting a job in a nightclub foam party where I had to scoop up real life human poos off the dance floor at the end of the night with a dustpan and a spatula and then got stranded there with no money and had to live on one packet of Cool Blue Doritos for six nights by rationing myself to two in the morning and two for dinner, and even that went tits up when I came back one day and found a mouse had peed on them.

'Hahahahahhahahaha!' laughed Murphy. 'They should make your life into a film, Shizshoz! SHIRAZ BAILEY WOOD THE MOVIE!'

'A bloody horror film! That's what it sounds like to me!' tutted my mother, giving me one of her best, 'I know you're my flesh and blood but Shiraz you're a total bloody embarrassment' faces.

'The thing is,' I said to everyone, going all red, 'all that stuff only sounds bad when you say it all together like that!' Well everyone just burst out laughing then and made sarcastic remarks. OK, everyone aside from my Wesley who didn't really say anything 'cos none of these adventures Cava-Sue mentioned involved Wes 'cos we were split up for ages last year. In fact at that time Wes was going out with that mutant from the planet swampdonkey, Susan bloody Douvall, or 'Sooz' as she's known. Sooz who works in Boots and spends all day selling bum ointment and intimate vaginal wipes. Sooz, who – instead of jumping in my grave the moment me and Wes split up – could maybe have used her time better flexing her 30%-off staff Boots discount card on some GHDs and a big tub of Sleek It Down serum, 'cos her hair looks all fuzzy like tramps' armpits! And it's not that I'm jealous of Sooz or nothing for having gone out with my Wes, 'cos I'm NOT. Wes says it weren't much fun seeing her anyway, in fact he was thinking about me all the time. Well Wes always says that, bless him. And I'm sure at least some of the time he must have been thinking 'Oh baby Jesus, Lord above why am I not with Shiraz and why am I now going out with a bird with such out-of-control hair that we ain't allowed on the premier balcony down Vue cinema 'cos everyone else wants their money back 'cos she obscures the view of the movie?' HAHAHAHAHHA!

Oh I don't mean this really, I'm being awful.

My Wes looked well handsome tonight. He had on his pale-blue, stripy Penguin polo shirt and his dark-navy True Religion jeans and some fresh white Nikes and a black baseball hat and his gold chain. My Wes looks nice, when he makes an effort. He looks like a slob sometimes though, when he's just hanging about the house playing Nintendo, I have to tell him to bloody get dressed! That bloody Nintendo does my head right in sometimes. One thing's for sure, my mother loves Wes more every single day he's alive. Especially when he turned up tonight and got well stuck into the birthday buffet, 'cos mother was fretting she'd bought too much. Oh my dayz, he even ate all the pork and apricot party *vol au vents* that my mother only shoved in the trolley to make up her Iceland 'five for £5' offer, even though the picture on the box made the pork bit look like old boiled snot with bum droppings in.

'Mmmm, Diane! These are well nice, innit!' Wesley said, heaping them on his plate along with a handful of cheesy footballs and a big thick ham sandwich which was giving me the bumshudders 'cos it was made from that ham in a can stuff with big lumps of yellow jelly stuck all over it. The sort of ham that only appears at Christmas and birthdays and the rest of the time is eaten only by Satan himself, after a hard day's graft down his firey pit.

'Oh Wes, I can always rely on you to pull your weight!' my mother said, loading his plate with more mini pork pies and mini sausages on sticks. Actually, now I come to think of it, my whole bloody birthday buffet was made of pig, well aside from the cake which I'm sure probably had an old hoof in it somewhere under the buttercream icing.

When it came to pressie time everyone gathered around and my mother gave me a card from her and my dad with a £25 Top Shop voucher in it!

'We've not got a bloody clue what you want, love, so

you can treat yourself!' she said. Bless her! I'm going to buy myself an amazing fancy going-out dress with it! Something short and a bit sexy I reckon. Something to go clubbing in! Well, if my Wesley ever wants to go out clubbing again. He always wants to stay in these days. Never mind, I'll go with Carrie instead. I'll just bloody ignore what Wes says about me hanging about with Carrie so much.

Wes reckons I'd be better off not hanging around with Carrie Draper, what with her having been in trouble with the police and everyone knowing. Wes keeps saying that Carrie is a bloody liability and he's not trying to be like my dad or nothing but he just loves me and he don't want me to get into no more trouble. Wes says that Carrie is bad news, and she's been lucky so far but her luck will run out one day and I KNOW HE'S GOT A POINT. But that's the thing, he ain't my dad and I'll do what I want and oh it's my birthday so I'm not going to think about this any more.

So then Cava-Sue and Lewis gave me their gift. The first bit was a big thick book which was called *Kick-Ass Women in History: A Beginners Guide to Feminism* by Angela Spout. Well Murphy let out a big fake snore when he saw it and my mother just sighed and said, 'Oh, Cava-Sue?! You could have got Shiraz something worth reading, like a proper good book. 'Ere hasn't Tiffany Poole the glamour model who is married to Peter Flazio the footballer got a new novel out at the moment? *Forever*

Love it's called! I saw it on the telly! It's a bestseller y'know!?' Well, Cava-Sue hissed and made a face and said that the Tiffany Poole books ain't exactly what she'd call a proper good book. No, the book she'd given me was all about great role models, kick-ass women, like Queen Elizabeth the First and Hilary Clinton and Madonna, and not forgetting Joan of Arc – who, Cava-Sue reminded everyone, was BURNED at the STAKE in 1431 at the age of nineteen for leading the French Army to several bloody victories while channelling visions from God!

Well no one said much after she said that, until my dad mumbled, 'Well she sounds like a right laugh,' and everyone started laughing except for my sister. Well Cava-Sue just made a loud tut sound then and gave me my second present. It was a small box with a ribbon around it. Inside was this small white plastic cup thing. It looked like the top off the Anchor squirty cream or a tiny egg cup or something.

'What is it?' I said to her.

'It's the most amazing thing ever!' said Cava-Sue.

'It's quite bendy!' I said, squishing down the sides of it. 'What is it!?'

'It's going to change your life for ever! It's going to change the planet, Shiraz!' said Cava-Sue, proper triumphantly.

'But what is it?' said my mother, peering at it, getting her glasses out of her bag.

'Yeah, what is it?' said everyone, staring at the little cup.

'It's a mooncup!' said Cava-Sue proudly.

'A whatcup!?' I said.

'A mooncup! It's a re-usable, environmentally friendly, menstruation device!' announced Cava-Sue. 'So women don't have to pollute the oceans with our waste products! You use it, then you wash it out and use it again the next month!'

'Oh my dear life,' said my mother, stepping backwards, holding on to the sink for support. 'That's not what I think it is, is it? You don't . . . shove that thing in your . . . I mean . . . ? Cava-Sue, have you gone beserk?'

'HahahahahhahahhahahAMAZING! It's a re-usable tampax!!!' laughed Murphy, almost dying with delight. Ritu tried to hide her entire face behind a plate of vol au vents.

'Mother!' quacked Cava-Sue. 'We all have to face up to our environmental legacy, yknow! Do have any idea how many tampon innertubes are floating about in the Pacific Ocean right now? Do you? Eighty-seven MILLION!'

'Flipping heck? Which poor git had to count all those?' said my dad, munching a pork pie in a matter-of-fact manner, as if years of living in a small house with three women had proper warped his ideas of inappropriate and appropriate conversation.

'No one COUNTS them father, that's just official statistics!' says Cava-Sue, 'It's on the internet!'

Well, now my mother had something to get her teeth stuck into. This is one of her favourite subjects.

23

'Oh, the bloody internet!' she tutted. 'Everything is on the internet these days! That internet thing causes more trouble than it's worth! I don't know why it's allowed!? I reckon half the folk using it are paedophiles and Arab folk wanting to do bombings! They should ban the internet they should! They should turn the internet off!'

Cava-Sue looked at my mother like she was an alien off the Planet Zarg. 'Mother, they can't turn the internet off,' she said, sighing. 'There ain't one big central switch in Number Ten Downing Street that says INTERNET ON/INTERNET OFF! It don't work like that!'

'Well there bleeding well should be!' says my mother, 'This country is going to the dogs. The police ain't got no control any more!'

By this point Wesley was doing sign language over at Murph along the lines of, 'Wanna get the Nintendo out?'

'Mother,' said Cava-Sue. 'If this country is going to the dogs, why are you having a go at me for trying to make things better?!'

'Well, why are YOU having a go at me for speaking my mind!' said my mother, swigging from her glass of Lambrella. 'People like me today can't speak their minds! We're too scared 'cos of all this bloody civil liberty nonsense!'

By this point neither my mother or Cava-Sue appeared to be in the same argument, but they were both pretty cross.

'OK you two, come on! We've all had a drink! Let's not

forget that this is supposed to be a party!' I shouted. Well Cava-Sue looked at my mother, and my mother looked at Cava-Sue's mooncup and she started to laugh. And then Cava-Sue's lip started to wobble and she started laughing too. It's hard to stay angry when one of you is waving a mooncup about.

You've got to say one thing about my family. They are mental as anything but they're still bare jokes sometimes, innit.

And, as ever, Wesley Barrington Bains II saved the day totally by producing his pressie from his pocket. It was a small box wrapped in shiny, silver paper. Inside it was a black velvet box. A ring box! Well Cava-Sue let out a gasp when she spotted it and my dad sort of looked proper uncomfy and my mother . . . well my mother's face lit up all happy as if someone had just told her the Channel Tunnel had finally been blocked up and no more foreigns were coming to Britain, ever.

'Wesley!?' I says, looking at the box. 'What is it?'

'Open it,' he said, looking all mushy at me.

'Yeah, open it!' shouts my mother, nearly ripping the box out of my hand and doing it for me. So I opened up the box slowly and inside was . . . a small silver heart.

It was a gorgeous, solid silver heart trinket to go on my charm bracelet. I stared at it and let out a quiet sigh of relief. Because for one stupid bloody moment I'd thought that Wes had maybe gone a bit mental and, well, y'know, BOUGHT ME A RING . . . y'know, a bloody serious ring. Oh that's mental, I know, I'm only nineteen years old. I'm far too young for any of that wedding stuff and me and Wes both know that . . . don't we?!

'What's that?!' said my mother, staring at it.

'It's a charm . . . for my charm bracelet!' I said.

'It's got "Shiraz Bailey Wood" engraved on one side,' said Wesley. 'And "Nineteen Years Old" engraved on the other side, innit.' Wesley looked well pleased with himself.

So I stuck my arms round his waist and gave him a kiss, just on the face though, 'cos my whole family were watching us.

'Oh? It's a trinket? For your bracelet?' said my mother. To be honest she looked well disappointed. 'Well, ain't that nice?' she said.

'Yeah, it's lovely,' I said, staring at it, 'cos it properly was. He's sweet my Wes. His pressies are always proper thoughtful.

Anyway soon afterwards everyone was going mad playing *Guitar Hero*. As usual my mother started off saying there's no way she would play, but as usual she couldn't resist and did 'Sweet Child of Mine' by Guns 'N' Roses, which is always funny 'cos she proper watches the screen close up and nearly widdles herself a bit every time she even gets one note right!

'But how does it know!?' she shouts, 'How does it know!!? Ooh this thing is so clever!'

And so eventually all the different pig-related food

products were eaten and Cava-Sue went and put Fin into his cot 'cos it was well past his bedtime and he was screaming the house down with his sore ear again. Then Clement and my dad started having a little 'nip' from Dad's bottle of Aldi 10,000 Sporrans Special Blended whiskey. And soon Nan made us call a minicab to take her and Clement home 'cos Clement was over-exciting himself playing Metallica.

Well at this point I sneaked off upstairs with my birthday presents. I need an early night 'cos I've got another day of babysitting tomorrow and three babies crying don't half jar your head.

To be honest, I've just been looking through Cava-Sue's book about amazing women like Condoleeza Rice and Oprah Winfrey and Charlotte Bronte, who made their lives into massive adventures, and I don't know why but I'm feeling a tiny bit . . . well . . . sad, to be honest. It's weird, I know, 'cos it's my birthday and I had such a nice day, but it just feels like I've had all my adventures over the last few years and now it's time to be a grown-up and be sensible. It feels like nothing mad will happen again. In fact, sometimes I look at my life and I think that it's all gone a bit wrong 'cos. . . . Wooooooooah, hang on a minute, Shiraz! Come on, we've all had a drink, ain't we! You're not thinking straight. I'm putting the light off now. In the morning it'll all be all right. I know it will.

WEDNESDAY 5TH OCTOBER

Today, after the babies had been picked up, I mopped the biggest, stickiest patches of Cow and Gate Apple and Pear Medley off my hoodie and dabbed the baby spew off my jeans, slapped on some lip-gloss and took our Penny for a walk over to Carrie's house. I needed cheering up to be honest 'cos the day had been well long. I had a bit of a baby 'smackdown' situation on my hands. My nephew Fin has decided he don't like Kezia's little girl Tiq ever since she crawled up and wacked him about the face with her Iggle Piggle. She was just saying hello. Well Fin took the right hump. He's a sensitive child is our Fin, y'know, even if he is chunky and bald and angry-looking, like a bouncer down at Eclipse in Romford.

Anyway, Fin didn't want to be in the same room as Tiq today and he screamed like he was under martian attack whenever she bloody looked at him. Oh and to make matters worse Tiq's going through a 'biting grown-ups' phase. Kezia warned me about this when she dropped her off on her way to the maternity clinic. ''Ere Shiz,' Kezia says, 'Watch her! She's like one of them pythons what you see on *I'm A Celebrity Get Me Out of Here!*' Well I laughed about that until I was reading Tiq a story later and the bloody thing sinks her fangs in me and almost draws blood! Aggggggggh!

So, what with all the biting and smacking and chucking of apple mush and bleak incidents involving baby bumgravy and nappies, it has been a VERY LONG DAY INDEED, even if I am getting five pound an hour per kid, which ain't bad at all. And it's cash in hand, so I'm not paying any of that tax wotsit stuff or nothing, innit? I'm saving it all up in a box under my bed. But honest to god, the only good bit about looking after a baby as far as I can see is that they sometimes fall asleep. And for that half hour they look like little cherubs, so cute you could almost nibble them and you don't have to worry about the little things being hungry or thirsty or hot or cold or lying in their own wee or poo or having trapped wind or even having meningitis that might kill them stone dead in about twenty minutes flat without any symptoms. 'Cos, OH MY DAYZ, babies are a proper worry!

The daft thing is all you have to do NOT to end up with one FOREVER is either take a pill or use some other type of contraceptive device thingy wotnot. EASY PEASY!! So why did so many girls in my class end up having one?? Soon Kezia's gonna have two!!! She must be mental. I was sat there for half an hour this afternoon with Tiq cuddled into my lap asleep, letting out little snores, and Fin in his cot snoozing too and I stuck on *Loose Women* on ITV1, which always cheers me up, especially today 'cos those mad old bats were all in a line talking about how their 'pelvic floor muscles' went all loose after they had kids, so now they widdle themselves in Sainsbury sometimes by accident. OH MY DAYZ, this being a woman lark is a right barrel of laughs, innit? It got me thinking about how hard being a girl is compared to being a boy. 'Cos when you're a girl there's all sorts of little shocks along the way, ain't there? You've just got to roll with them or you'd go nuts.

I mean, if you're not putting up with your period coming every month, well you're worrying about it not coming at all, and getting up the duff by accident. And if you have the baby you might even end up like Cava-Sue with her post-natal depression gubbins, dressing in nothing but your pyjamas for six months afterwards and getting earache off the manager of Netto for breast-feeding by the chicken counter! Boys don't have to put up with any of this, do they? And then ... THEN ... when all your years of having babies are over you might start going all bonkers like Carrie Draper's mum, who Carrie reckons is going through the menopause even though she's not that old – in her forties or something. But Carrie reckons her mum's having proper bad mood swings, which make her want to chuck a plate of Kung Po Chicken at Barney Draper's head in Spirit of Siam restaurant. Apparently Barney dared to suggest that Maria's red dress, red coat, red shoes and red handbag outfit made her look a bit like Mrs Santa Claus. Well, Maria Draper went proper full-on barmy and hasn't spoken to Barney for five whole days. Carrie reckons it's all down to her hormones. Carrie says hormones are why men rule the world and why us girls are the weaker sex – because we're full of hormones . . . they make us act daft and make silly choices. Carrie says there ain't nothing we can do about that.

I don't want to make stupid choices though. I want to do amazing things and live a proper brilliant life. I want to travel and see stuff and have adventures like the women in that Kick-Ass Women book. I don't want to just look after babies, even if people do think I'm the babysitting queen. I reckon I could do something more. This is as far as I got with my thinking 'cos then Tiq woke up and bit me on the bloody arm again.

It took me and silly fat Pen bloody ages to get to Carrie's house tonight 'cos Penny walks so slow. She's pretty big at the moment. I won't call her fat 'cos fat ain't a nice word, but it is true to tell she has had limited success in her 'battle with the bulge' and is well round. In fact, she looks a lot like a slow-motion brown pig. Murph says cruel things about Pen like I should be careful with her down the park in case a crowd of partially sighted kids mistake her for a bouncy castle. But honest to baby Jesus. I've trying again since I got back from Ibiza to get Pen down to a slimline slinky weight but it has been a complete FIASCO. Me and my mother tried AGAIN putting Pen on those Purina low fat biscuits, that the vet kept nagging us about, but it didn't work. No joy whatsoever. The vet's only hacked off 'cos the leg fell off his examination table last time Pen sat on it. No sense of humour, that's his problem. Anyways we tried the biscuits and poor Pen was only allowed about an egg cup's worth of the bloody things and no special treat Pepperami Firesticks or Lion Bars or Pukka Pies or anything. Her food supply was on LOCKDOWN. And this worked for about three days and then as usual she started breaking free and wandering down Thundersley Road blagging that she was a stray and begging on doorsteps. I decided to take action, so stuck up little posters on the lampposts from our doorstep all the way to Londis with a message that read:

CITIZENS OF THUNDERSLEY ROAD – DO NOT FEED THIS DOG!

I even put a little photo of Pen's face underneath it, looking all guilty, like on Rogue's Gallery on *Crimewatch*. Carrie made me them on her MacBook Air. Well the posters worked for a bit, but to be honest none of the Brunton-Fletcher kids can read anyway and they all proper love Staffies so the moment one of the twins thieved a box of Limited Edition Peanut Kit Kats from Bargain Booze, well we never saw our Pen for two days. Eventually she came back even fatter, with peanut gunk encrusted all around her snout. HONEST BRUV, I give up. I said this to Pen today, I did, I said, 'PENNY, I GIVE UP.' But Pen weren't listening to me 'cos she was off by the bandstand finishing an old Ginsters chicken tikka pasty she'd found behind a bush.

* * *

When we got to Draperville, Carrie had just got home from a driving lesson with her dad. I knew this 'cos her little Golf was parked all wonky in the driveway and there was gravel chucked all over the place and her dad Barney was sat on the side of the ornamental pond with his head in his hands and all the colour drained from his face like he'd had a life-threatening experience.

'Hi Mr D, how's it going?' I said to him. Barney tried to say hello, but then started wheezing and got out his asthma inhaler and took a few sharp blasts. Then he put his head in his hands again. Carrie's driving obviously isn't getting any better. She's already had one test which she failed FIVE MINUTES OUT OF THE TEST CENTRE for emergency stopping in the middle of the road and adjusting the central mirror. Carrie told me she only wanted to re-do her lip-gloss 'cos the examiner had said she had to drive in the direction of Stanley Park Playing Grounds, where the Millwall under-21s sometimes hang out doing football coaching for kids. 'Well I weren't driving past looking like a yeti, was I, Shiz!?' she says to me, straight-faced. Carrie don't even try to be bare jokes, she just is.

So I left Barney to it and walked up the drive, past Carrie's car and that's when I notice the right front wingmirror was missing.

'Oh my gosh!' I says.

Barney Draper pipes up behind me, 'Parallel parking, Shiraz! Parallel bloody parking! How hard is it to get a car that small in a four-metre space!?' He looked well depressed. Poor Barney.

Just then Carrie's mother strutted out the house wearing a burgundy velour tracksuit and gave Barney a black look and jumped into her jeep. She didn't say hello to either of us and then she drove off. Maybe Carrie's right about her?

Me and Penny went in the house and went upstairs where Carrie was in her bedroom, lying on her king-sized bed, painting her nails pink and watching *My Super Sweet 16* on MTV. She was watching this girl called Rochelle Du Lane whose daddy had bought her Usher for a birthday present. Yes, that's right, Usher! No, not to hang out with, or anything like that! Just to sing for her. Let's face it Usher singing Happy Birthday To You is still proper SOLID GOLD amazing, innit?! Well it happens Rochelle didn't think so 'cos she spent the whole day moaning saying she wanted Jay Z instead, mardy cow! I watched it for a bit with my mouth open, starting to feel quite jealous. That's the thing about shows like this, ain't it. You get to the end and think, 'Oh my days, my life's a right load of crap compared to that.'

I watched as far as when Rochelle's daddy gave her the keys to her own silver speedboat, then I decided to pick up a magazine and look the other way.

'I can't believe these spoiled bints!' Carrie sighed to me while lying on her back with her MacBook Air on her chest looking at TopShop.com for new shoes. Carrie is looking well pretty at the moment. All the worry of the prison thing has made her well slim and she's had some blonde hair extensions put into her hair so it looks longer and thicker like a mermaid's. She looks properly gorgeous, like Colleen McCloughlin, these days. People say that when we go down Goodmayes together. They say ''Ere, don't I know you? Are you that whatshername . . . ?' Carrie just giggles, loving it, and then they turn to me and say, 'So are you her assistant or something?' CHEEKY GITS! Do I look like someone's assistant?

'These parents are ruining their kids!' Carrie said now, pointing at the telly.

'I know,' I said.

'It don't do them no favours, I reckon,' Carrie said. 'I'm glad my dad always made me get part-time jobs. It taught me the value of money!'

Well, I nearly wet myself then 'cos Carrie was trying to make out that the time she worked in Barney's office at Draper Hydration for two weeks, basically moving the same invoice, round the same desk, in a three-hundred-and-sixty-degree motion while watching Kate Modern on Bebo, was in any way 'work'! HAHAHAHAHAHAHHA HAHAH!

Carrie has no idea about the value of money! Carrie ain't ever had a proper job, well aside from in Ibiza and LOOK how that ended! But I didn't want to say that as it was cruel, 'cos to be honest it's going to be well hard for Carrie to get a real job now 'cos she's been in trouble with the police. I mean, OK, she wasn't charged or nothing but everyone knows about it 'cos she was on *Sky News* and in *The Sun*. And when she flew home she was a little bit famous for a while and she gave an interview to *The News of The World* for four grand where she was standing about in a bikini and high heels under the headline 'MY DRUG-SMUGGLING IBIZAN PRISON HELL'. She wasted the money on handbags and shoes pretty much right away, too.

To be honest, I'm a bit worried about Carrie. When we both got back from Ibiza she was well giddy from all the 'media attention'. She even went on BBC Radio Essex on a talk show and was on *London Tonight* news, but now things have gone a bit quiet. In fact, no one phones her up any more at all. It's like her tiny bit of fame is over. Not that being in trouble with the police is 'famous' anyway, is it? My Wesley says it isn't. He says it's more like a big black mark against you. He ain't trying to be nasty, he's just telling the truth.

Anyway, the one thing Carrie is certain about is that she reckons now for definite that she was meant to be famous 'cos she well enjoyed all the attention and getting her makeup done for photo-shoots and talking to reporters about her life. And she knows she don't want to be a professional singer any more. Carrie wants to just be a 'personality' and build up her own multimillion pound empire where she does reality shows and has her own perfume and knicker range and writes books and appears on magazine covers and releases a workout DVD, a bit like Tiffany Poole the model who is married to Peter Flazio who plays for Chelsea. Carrie isn't totally sure how you go about doing that though. She reckons the first stage is by 'getting exposure' on TV or something. I mean, last week I called Carrie up 'cos the council were having a 'Young Women Starting in Business' day at Ilford Town Hall and I reckoned we should go down there together and see if they had any advice for girls like us who were proper bright but didn't have many qualifications or whatever. But Carrie wouldn't come. 'No bloody way!' Carrie says to me. 'I'm not getting one of them normal jobs, Shiz! The only business I'm interested in is showbusiness! I want this so badly. I want it 110%.'

Tonight Carrie was making a list of stuff she's going to apply for this October and November. She's proper confident that by January next year she'll be on Living TV or ITV2 with a reality show and be at least a D-List celeb. Carrie's started getting this newspaper delivered every week called *The Stage*, which has lots of adverts in it for singers and dancers and auditions for reality shows. She's also signed herself up with a site called *www.ucanbefamous.com* which text messages you if a band or a DJ needs 'crowds' to dance in their videos. Carrie got twenty quid last week to dance under a sprinkler in the EZ Riderz *Crank Your Booty* video. It was on Channel U and everything. You can proper make out the back of Carrie's head if you know which one she is.

''Ere Shiz,' Carrie said to me tonight, 'I'm going to apply to be on *Love Cruise* on ITV2.' That's the one where they put a load of young people on a boat and film you getting drunk and getting off with each other! It's well funny! Will you come with me to the audition to keep me company?'

'Yeah. Suppose so. If I'm not working,' I said. 'I've got a job you know?!'

'Ha!' Carrie laughed. 'Shiraz, you can't call sitting in the house looking after folk's babies a job. That ain't a job.'

I felt like saying to Caz that she couldn't call lying about on her skinny ass dreaming of being famous, letting her dad put money into her account once a month anything to be proud of EITHER but I couldn't face an argument 'cos we've been getting along proper well recently since Ibiza.

For the rest of the night me, Carrie, Penny and Alexis – Carrie's chihuahua – lay on the bed watching *High School Musical 3* on knock-off DVD. Carrie's dad got it for her from some Vietnemese bloke down Tesco car park. Lord alive, that Zac Ephron ain't getting any more ugly as he gets older, innit? He's still so proper choong my eyes go a bit wonky just looking at him. Me and Caz were also flipping through her mother's copy of *Hello!* magazine 'cos it was a Tiffany Poole birthday special issue with all the photos of her thirtieth birthday party.

OH MY DAYZ! Tiffany Poole's birthday was pretty

amazing. She had a big luxury yacht sailing down the Thames in London and all her family and close showbiz friends were there.

All Tiffany's friends are pop stars or models or people out of *EastEnders*. All the girls are skinny and tanned and size zero and all the men are either footballers or have been in *Hollyoaks* and Tiffany's children are all gorgeous too. And the party food was made by Johnny Olivetti the celebrity chef and they had oysters and sushi and there was definitely no Iceland snot and bumdroppings *vol au vents* or ham in jelly either. And Tiffany's entertainment was a live personal appearance from McFly singing all of their hit songs followed by a three-hundred grand firework display near the Houses of Parliament. Yeah, Tiffany's party most definitely – unlike Shiraz Bailey Wood's birthday – did NOT feature an old-age pensioner drunk on whisky playing *Guitar Hero III* while two women bickered about a re-usable tampon.

'Tiffany Poole has the best life ever, don't she?' Carrie said, 'I'm so jealous. I'd do anything to swap with her, wouldn't you?'

'Mmmn, yeah,' I sighed. And y'know I'm not usually that bothered by the whole celeb thing, I'm all about keeping it real, but I had to admit it, Tiffany's life just looked cool.

* * *

I went down Ilford Xchange with Kezia today. We took Tiq and Collette Brown's little boy Rudi with us too in their prams. I said I'd take Rudi for five hours while Collette was working down at the new tanning salon she's been setting up with her mate Tasha. Tanorife, it's called. A bit like Tenerife the holiday island, except you don't need to fly to Tenerife to get brown 'cos you can book some sessions at Tanorife instead. Cava-Sue says it's depressing that Collette is 'squandering the world's electricity supply turning Essex girls the colour of chicken tikka masala marinaded Oompa-Loompas and encouraging skin cancer just to promote a warped Western world concept that tanned skin is beautiful'. Oh my dayz, she needs to lighten up. Cava-Sue says what's wrong with being pale anyway!? She would say that though 'cos her and Lewis are emos and their skin is so white it's actually almost blue when you get up close! Murph says that's just the 'sadness within their souls coming up to the surface. HA HA HA HA HA! Me and Murph laughed for ages after he said that and then Cava-Sue rolled up a copy of *NME* magazine and whacked him with it, and my mother told us all to bloody grow up.

I said to Cava-Sue last night that if she's one of them 'feminists' like she claims, well she should be supporting Collette for being a single mum with her own business. That's a proper 'kick ass' thing for a woman to do I reckon.

Cava-Sue just wrinkled her nose then and said what she'd like to know is WHERE Collette gets the money from to buy all the sunbeds, 'cos Collette used to hang about with some well shady blokes. Blokes with skinheads and squashed noses who drive 4x4 Land Rovers with tinted windows.

Well I couldn't deny this, 'cos it was true. In fact that's how Collette ended up having Rudi, and no one knows for sure who Rudi's dad is, 'cos Collette is proper adamant she ain't naming him on the birth certificate even if she proper gets it in the neck BIG TIME from the child support bods whenever she needs money. I don't think I could just leave it blank. It looks a bit slack, don't it? I'd be tempted just to write something like Zac Ephron or Jay Z just to be a bit glamorous.

Me and Kez pushed the prams down past Tanorife today and popped our heads in quickly to say hello. It looks well posh! There's vertical beds and horizontal sun beds and you can even have a spray tan thing where you stand in a booth in the nuddy and it wooshes you with spray on both sides, then you dry all lovely and golden brown. Well, it's meant to. Later on Kezia told me that when Collette first got the booths delivered she stuck all the liquid tan in the wrong tubes so they were only squirting the left half of customer's bodies and leaving the right half totally white! Kezia says people were going proper schizoid screaming mental at Collette 'cos they were left walking about Ilford two different colours like Two Face from the Batman movies! Me and Kezia were having a right laugh about that today when we were sat on the wall outside Greggs eating our lunch.

Kezia had a Cornish pasty and an iced yum yum and I had a jumbo sausage roll and a strawberry doughnut. I felt a bit bad afterwards though 'cos I know it wasn't very good for me, in fact, I knew if I'd bought it down the supermarket it would have had red traffic light stickers all over it saying WARNING HIGH FAT AND SUGAR. I'm only bothered 'cos ever since I got back from Ibiza and got back with my Wesley I'm feeling a bit, well, more 'round'. In fact this morning when I went to put on one of my hoodies I haven't worn since I lived in London, it was sort of ... 'snug' on the arms. I AM STARTING TO GET BINGO WINGS!!!! I ran downstairs and told my mother and Cava-Sue and they both found it very amusing.

'Ha ha ha ha! We've all got them! They run in the family!' Then they both put their hands in the air and started wobbling their dimply arm-fat at me until I had a panic attack and needed to go and lie on my bed!

Aaaaaagh! I can't let this happen! It's all those bloody Chicken Jalapeño pizzas me and Wes keep ordering on our 'cosy nights in'. And it don't bloody help that Georgos in the pizza shop is a mate of Wes and keeps putting free extra slices of banoffi pie and barbecue chicken wings in the bag too!

'Aw, I think it's well nice you feel comfy to just be yourself, Shiz,' Kezia says to me today. 'You've got your fella now. You don't need to try so hard any more, innit?'

Well that freaked me out to be honest. I don't want to stop trying. And have I really 'got my fella' now? For ever? I don't want to tell people I'm not one hundred per cent sure 'cos everyone is so bloody beaming with joy happy for us.

Me and Kezia had a right laugh today, just wheeling the buggies about town. Kez is well funny when she's pregnant 'cos she is proper 'out and proud', with her crop top resting above her bare belly and her trackie bottoms under the bump. Kez's hair is currently pure, bright orange, 'cos she can't dye it when she's pregnant, so she's a proper unmissable sight in the mall. Kez acts different when she's up the duff. It's like all the hormones are sloshing about her head making her think deeper, plus she can't move about as quick so basically she's just a more chilled out Kezia Marshall who's into eating and chatting, not the Kezia we saw in Ibiza, who was basically hammered drunk on Aftershock and Red Bull every night and dancing on tables.

Kezia was chatting a lot today about her new baby. Kez says she's been proper fretting about how she's going to manage with two babies 'cos having one is hard enough. She says she's just going to have to manage though, 'cos she's gone and done it now and that's that ain't it? Kez says she's trying not to get all stressed out about things 'cos there's girls far worse off than her, like her next door neighbour Amiri who came to England last year from Iraq 'cos of the war. Kez says that Amiri is twenty-one and she's got three kids. Kez say that Amiri and her husband Uday can't see any of their families back home any more 'cos they both escaped from Iraq and their families didn't and Amiri thinks they might be dead. Kez says that Amiri has to get all her kids down three flights of stairs in Block D of Kez's high rise, when the lift is broken, carrying her pram while wearing her full head-to-floor burkha. At least Kez has got her mother Marlita to help her with Tiq. Amiri doesn't have anyone. I thought about Amiri for a while afterwards and it made me sad, 'cos I see my whole family every day and though sometimes it does my head in, they're always there around me.

Kezia and me wandered down by the market with our prams and had a look at the knock-off Gucci and Louis Vuitton handbags, like Tiffany Poole has, except their ones are made in India by tiny little orphans. I saw it in a magazine, shocking it was.

So we're looking through the fake bags when this old lady came up and takes a look in our prams and tells us we both had beautiful babies! Well I tried to say that Rudi wasn't mine but she didn't seem to believe me. 'He ain't my baby!' I said. 'This is just my job! I'm finishing my A-Levels and having a career!' I says to her. But the old woman just smiled at me and shook her head like she didn't understand and wandered off.

'Yeah, whatever, Shiz, shut up, you'll have your own by this time next year,' said Kezia.

Well, honest to god this made my bingo wings shudder 'cos she weren't even kidding. I am not having a baby, right? That ain't happening! I don't mind hanging about the mall with a pram now and then. But I ain't doing it forever. NO WAY.

It was quite a warmish night tonight, so after I dropped Rudi back at Tanorife, me and Kez walked back to Goodmayes. Kez was chatting about giving birth this time around and how she wants to have her new baby in hospital, 'cos last time she did it on the floor in her flat with her sisters holding an ankle each and it was well uncomfortable. Kezia says this time she wants all the drugs she can get hold of. In fact Kez says this time she's checking herself into hospital a week early and they can start pumping her full of the drugs 'cos she won't have had a single Bacardi Breezer since Ibiza and she's dying to get well clattered off her head. So I asked Kez who was coming for the birth this time and she said her mother would be, deffo.

'What about the dad?' I says.

Kez went quiet for a bit and said that he'd probably not be able to make it. So I asks Kezia, gently mind, if she was going to tell me who the dad of her new baby was, 'cos so far she has been all secretive about it. Well Kezia thought for a while then she says to me, 'Look, Shiz, you gotta keep this quiet right? 'Cos only he knows and he ain't told his family or nothing.'

So I says, ' 'Course, Kez. Swear on our Penny's life, I do.' And that's the best promise I could ever give.

' 'Cos the thing is, he says he loves me, right?' said Kez. 'And we've even talked about getting engaged!'

'Bloody hell, Kez, this is serious!' I said. And the minute I said it I felt a bit silly 'cos what is more serious than growing a baby inside you?

'The thing is, I want my baby to have a dad, Shiz! A proper dad with a name I can write on the certificate thing. I don't want it to be blank like Collette's babyfather.'

'I know Kez,' I said.

So then she whispered the name in my ear. And to be honest it was a name me and Carrie had been wondering about for months.

Clinton Brunton-Fletcher.

Our friend Uma's brother. Uma's awful brother Clinton. The one who is now in Chelmsford Prison doing five years for cocaine supplying. He could be out in two years apparently, if he keeps out of trouble. Oh God, Clinton never keeps out of trouble, though, does he? Maybe he will if he's got something to get out for? Is that bad or good though? Maybe it's better for everyone when he's in?

I walked home the rest of the way to Thundersley Road thinking about what she'd told me. Oh my dayz, Uma is going to get a right shock about this! If Clinton marries Kezia then Uma and Kez will be related. They'll be sister-in-laws! Kezia will be Kezia Brunton–Fletcher! And if Clinton adopts Kezia's little girl Tiq, who is actually Luther Drisdale's kid, well then Tiq's name will be Latanoyatiqua Marshall-Drisdale-Brunton-Fletcher!!! OMG that's nearly all the vowels and consonants in the alphabet! The Child Support Association is going to need some bigger forms with bigger spaces, innit?

I can't tell anyone Kezia's secret. Even if it is the best secret in the world ever.

THURSDAY 13TH OCTOBER

I went round my Wes's house tonight to watch a DVD and have my dinner cooked for me. Well that was the plan, but when I got round there, there were no cooking smells, and no DVD in sight. In fact Wes was sat in his armchair, still wearing his smelly work overalls playing *Grand Theft Auto IV* on-line with his mate Bezzie Kelleher. Bezzie was at home at his mum's house in Dawson Drive. They were both wearing their headsets chatting away to each other.

'Oh my life, Shiraz, is that the time?' Wes said to me when I walked in. 'I only sat down five minutes ago, innit!'

'Wesley! It's seven 'o clock!' I says. 'You were playing this at four, when I called you. Have you even ordered any food?'

'Eh?' he said to me, proper distracted again. 'What was that, innit?'

'Have you even ordered any food?' I said, well slowly, like Wesley was deaf or something.

'Hahahahahahah! Oh Bezzie, you plantpot!' Wes started howling pointing at the telly. 'How d'you mess that up!? It was obvious that blud with the hat was gonna merk ya, innit!'

I sat down on the sofa and picked up the pizza menu and sighed. I suppose I should be thankful Wes only plays his Nintendo sometimes. Not like Bezzie who is proper obsessed and plays it 24/7. I said this to Bezzie the other night when he came over.

' 'Ere Bez,' I said, 'Do you not think you're playing a bit too much *Grand Theft Auto*? Maybe you need to get a proper hobby or something, 'cos I don't reckon you're getting much fresh air. Your skin's looking a bit grey like you got one of them vitamin deficiency things or something? You need to get out and about a bit more, I reckon.'

Well, Bezzie just grunted when I said that. Then he says to me, 'I do get out and about a lot as it happens, THANK YOU SHIRAZ! I've just got back from the city limits where I've been delivering a parcel.'

I stared at Bezzie sadly when he said that.

'Mmmm, y'see in fairness, Bez,' I said, 'spending all day carrying out drug-running missions ain't really getting "out and about" is it? 'Cos it ain't happening

48

in REAL LIFE, is it? It's all happening on *Grand Theft Auto!* This is an example of you starting to blur "reality" with "non-reality", ain't it? This is what I'm sort of getting at.'

Well Bezzie didn't really say much to that because he was too busy taking out four assailants armed with machine guns who were lying in wait for him in an abandoned bowling alley. I know he heard me though, 'cos he proper scowled. Some people just can't handle me being real and having opinions can they? I'm only being true to myself though. At least I'm not saying it behind his back. (Actually, I say MUCH worse things behind Bezzie's back.)

I reckon Bezzie Kelleher is probably the only person in Essex NOT doing cartwheels of pure joy about me and my Wes getting back together. I know this 'cos one night last week I was in the kitchen making some coffee and I overheard Bezzie saying how much he missed Sooz coming round to the flat. Sooz! Susan bloody Douvall – Wesley's ex-girlfriend!

Well I didn't say anything at the time but honest to God, when I go to heaven I'm going to have to confess that the reason Bezzie's coffee tasted a bit funny that night was 'cos I stirred a spoonful of Bisto gravy granules into it!!! He is well in my bad books now. He has crossed a line!

My Wesley says to me tonight that maybe I shouldn't be so hard on Bezzie 'cos he reckons Bezzie is going through a proper life crisis. Wesley reckons that Bezzie was pretty sure he was going to be a famous rapper by now living in a mansion in Essex, with a hot-tub full of gorgeous black babes in jacuzzis pouring bottles of champagne over their heads, and a recording studio in the basement, like someone off *Cribs*. But that ain't really happened. Apparently Bezzie's been trying to lay down some tracks for the new Goodmayes Detonator album and it ain't going so brilliant. Bezzie reckons he's having some sort of writer's block scenario like all the great rappers go though at some point. Bezzie says he looks back at tracks like *Who Got Da Beef?* that he wrote three years ago and feels sad 'cos maybe his best rhyming days are behind him.

HAHAHAHAHA. Sorry but that is too jokes. Bezzie's even been wondering if maybe converting to Islam might give his writing a new direction 'cos it worked for Mos Def and Q Tip from A Tribe Called Quest. Wesley says Bezzie's been looking into becoming Muslim, but it turns out that would mean him praying five times a day, which is a well lot of praying, and to be honest he's just bought the entire seven seasons of *The Shield* on DVD boxset so he might watch that first. Oh, and apparently Bezzie is also a bit depressed 'cos it's proper hard for him to see his ex Carrie Draper going about Ilford looking all buff in her mini-skirts with her hair extensions 'cos it's taken Bezzie till now to realise what he's lost and he thinks he wants Carrie back.

I nearly choked on my banoffi pie when he said that. He is going insane I reckon.

'Wesley,' I says, 'Bezzie and Carrie split up nearly three and half years ago! Believe me bruv, Carrie has well moved on! And Wes, even if Cazza was suddenly going to have a change of heart, what's Bezzie got to offer her? He ain't on *Cribs* is he?! He ain't a famous rapper! He lives with his mother and Shane, their hundred-year-old King Charles spaniel. He's dropped out of college and had to sell the Vauxhall Nova with the silver wheel arches. He ain't got a job, he smokes bongs all day and his skin is grey 'cos he plays *Grand Theft Auto* 24/7 and don't ever get any fresh air!'

Well Wes said that he's never thought about it like that. Then he said maybe we need to invite Bezzie over to his flat a bit more so we could keep an eye on him. BRILLIANT. ME AND MY BIG GOB.

Me and Wes finished our pizza and lay on the sofa together watching the *EastEnders* repeat on BBC3. I wasn't really sure what was going on. I ain't caught the Sunday omnibus show for ages. As far as I could make out someone had a party in the Queen Vic and it wound up with everyone shouting and crying and one woman getting a good slap around the chops and crying even more. Actually I think this might happen in every episode of *EastEnders*. *EastEnders* is proper predictable, right? The same things happen all the time. Day after day. I started saying this to my Wes. I said, 'Oh my dayz, this show is always the same. It drives me mad sometimes!' But Wes didn't reply. And when I looked around at him I realised he was snoring. HE'D FALLEN ASLEEP! We were having a cosy night in and he played *Grand Theft Auto* for two hours and then fallen asleep! It's not the first time this has happened lately, either!

I sat there for a bit staring at him, sleeping like a little boy. I love Wesley's face when he's asleep, it's all soft and peaceful. His eyelashes flutter as he snores. I love him I do. He's my bloke. But then as I started flicking through the TV channels sitting on my own I started to feel proper bored. 'Cos honest to god, tonight weren't exactly a fun-filled evening in was it? In fact we haven't done anything fun for ages. It's always the same. Like we're living in *EastEnders*!

Just that moment, my phone started ringing in my bag. I leaned over the pile of pizza boxes and grabbed it. Carrie's picture was flashing on and off on the screen.

'All right, Shiz!' she said, proper chirpy. 'I didn't wake you up did I?'

'No,' I said. 'I'm at Wesley's flat. It's only 10.30pm. Why?!'

'Oh, right, I thought you were at home tonight. You're always in bed asleep early these days, innit?' She laughed. 'You're well boring!'

'No I am not!' I said. 'I'm the opposite of boring actually, Carrie Draper. I'm wild.'

'Ha! Yeah, right. When I called you up on your

birthday when your family were all having that party, you'd gone to bed! Boring cow!' snorts Carrie.

'I wanted to read my book!' I said.

'Hahahahahahah!! BORING!' howled Carrie.

'Oh, Whatever-Trevor,' I laughed, going a bit red 'cos I knew she might have a point. 'Anyway, what do you want? Did you just ring me up to insult me, 'cos I've got some crazy, mad, bonkers thing I need to be getting on with.'

'What like?' she says.

'Oh, well, erm,' I mumbled, 'There's a dinosaur documentary on the Discovery Channel in ten minutes. 'They're doing the Brontosaurus this week and that's my favourite.'

I'm watching a lot of random documentaries these days at Wesley's about stupid things. He's got all the Sky channels. Plus he's always bloody asleep.

'HAHAHAHAHHAHAHAHAH BRONTOSAURUSES!' laughed Carrie. 'WOOT WOOT! 'Ere, you wanna get a shout out on Westwood for that one! OK, well I better be quick then, one little question. What you doing next Thursday? Can you get off that babysitting thing? I'm going on an adventure! Wanna come with me?'

'What sort of adventure?' I said, keeping in mind that Carrie's last adventure wound up with us talking to each other through reinforced glass in an lbizan prison visiting room, and at one point Carrie getting a thorough and intimate body examination by a woman wearing surgical gloves.

'I'm going to audition for *Supermodel Unmasked*!' Carrie said. 'Y'know the show on ITV2!? The show where they find ten new potential supermodels and they put them in a house and do a photo-shoot of them every week and kick one off at the end of each show!? The one where the winner gets a modelling contract and a cover shoot for *Cosmopolitan* magazine! You know which one?'

'Yeah, 'course I do,' I said, 'I've watched it at yours lots of times. I didn't know you wanted to be a model?!'

'Yeah, big time I do,' said Carrie. 'And loads of famous people started off as models. Tiffany Poole started off as a model! Anyway, I *could* be a model! Loads of people always say that don't they?'

'Yeah, you're right they do,' I admitted.

'Well they're starting the pre-heats now for cycle five!' said Carrie, sounding proper giddy.

'The "preheats" for the "cycles"? What are you wittering on about?' I said.

'That's what they call it on *Supermodel Unmasked*. They're not auditions, they're "pre-heats". And each series is called a "cycle". That's the jargon ain't it? That's what Genevieve Shaw calls it!'

Oh god, I proper shuddered just thinking about Genevieve Shaw. She's that supermodel from New York who presents the show. She's well scary she is. She's about fifty years old but her face looks twenty-five! She's got dyed black hair and really muscly arms and big boobs which protrude right out with a big flat gap in the middle you could park a London taxi between! She always wears little white vests and white combat pants. Her catchphrase is, 'Walk! Walk! OK stop walking!' That's what she shouts at the girls when they're auditioning for her. She makes them walk up and down doing model poses, then she slags them off for not walking properly. How can you not walk properly? You put one foot in front of the other and move forward trying not to fall over! Walking is easy. Even Murphy can do 'walking', and I've been doing it since I was one.

'Will Genevieve Shaw be there at the audition?!' I said.

'Yeah, I think so!' said Carrie, 'Oh my God, Shiraz. She's a proper legend ain't she? I love her attitude. And she built her empire up from nothing, just like I'm going to! She was from a well dangerous part of Brooklyn in New York. We've got loads in common!'

I laughed a bit when Caz said that 'cos I knew she was calling me from within Draperville which has an electric fence, twenty-four-hour CCTV and a private firm who drive past every hour to check out if everything's fine. Somehow Carrie still reckons she's living in the ghetto.

'So, are you gonna come with me to show me some support, Shiz? Oh go on! Please!' she said. 'The auditions are at the O2 Arena in London! I'm going down Tanorife next Wednesday to get Collette to do my tan for me! Collette's got a new shade in called "Girl from Mars". It's like a deep apricot colour. It's for girls who want to take their tan to a new level of Mediterranean!

It's amazing! And I'm getting some more hair extensions in too! My mum's hairdresser has got some lovely new ones in from Lithuania. Proper soft they are! I'm going to look amazing! Please come, Shizza! I don't want to go on my own.'

'Hmmm. Next Thursday, you say?' I said.

'Next Thursday! Pleeaase!' she squeaked. ''Ere Shiz, imagine if I win this? Imagine how famous I'll be? I will be one of the most famous people in Britain!'

I looked across at my Wesley lying fast asleep with his foot resting in a carton of barbecue chicken wings. Suddenly a day out in London seemed like just what I needed.

'Yeah, reckon I'll come,' I said.

THURSDAY 20TH OCTOBER

Today was proper exciting 'cos me and Carrie went to London! We went to the O2 Arena near Greenwich so Caz could audition for *Supermodel Unmasked* with Genevieve Shaw!

Oh my gosh, it was a day filled with ups and downs and laughter and tears and joy and pain and that sort of what-not. Oh, and a bit somewhere in the day when me and Carrie ate McDonalds Happy Meals and finally got the free Disney Parrot Fandango toy drums we've been waiting for, 'cos they've been giving out the trumpets for weeks now. We were well bored with the trumpets by then but the drums were totally worth waiting for 'cos they had Orange Parrots on the side and we banged them and sang 'Goodmayes Girls Run Ting!' until we were told to 'Bloody grow up' by a McDonalds Team Leader with five gold stars on his shirt who was well arsey 'cos the power had clearly gone to his head and corrupted him. That's what Ms Bracket my old English teacher used to say to us. 'Power corrupts! And absolute power corrupts absolutely!' she'd say. She always said this when we were reading *King Lear* by Shakespeare which is all about people going a bit mental at the thought of being important.

I proper miss studying English with Ms Bracket. I used to learn new stuff every day. Useful stuff. Not that I don't learn stuff now, but it's mostly stuff to do with babies and bottles of milk formula and bum explosions. OK, today I learned a bit about how they make reality television. And a bit about the modelling industry. But I kind of wish I didn't know about that stuff. Not now, anyhow.

But I'm getting 'ahead of myself', which was another thing Ms Bracket used to say. I'll start at the beginning, yeah? So, I met Carrie at ten this morning by the ticket barriers at Goodmayes Station. Well, it was supposed to be ten but it was more like half past before Carrie made her personal showbiz appearance. Cheeky mare! And when she did turn up she didn't even say sorry! She just said, 'Oh, I had to get ready Shiraz! It took me ages! The fuse on my GHDs went so I had to get Mrs Raziq to change the plug.' Like this was a proper watertight excuse. Like Caz hadn't quite sussed that maybe getting her lazy ass out of her king-size bed earlier might have been helpful too! Anyway, I've got to hand it to Carrie, she looked proper beautiful today. Extra-specially beautiful. Like someone off *Hollyoaks* you might see going shopping in a *Heat* magazine 'Spotted' shoot or something. Sometimes I think if Carrie weren't my friend and I just saw her in ASDA, well I'd probably not like her on sight her 'cos I'd be well jealous of her body and just the way she always pulls her outfits together with all the things matching and looking pretty. I bloody love it when she does my makeup before we go out for a night 'cos she just proper turns me into a whole new Shiraz Bailey Wood. Like, ABRACADABRA. PIFF PAFF POOF!

Y'know, sometimes I feel proper sorry for boys, because they can't wear makeup without getting hassle. I mean, when you're a girl, even if you're minging you can well tart yourself up with a few powders and pencils, can't you? That's one good thing about being a girl, I reckon. You get a chance to make yourself look better. If you're a boy, you're just stuck with the face you've got, innit?

Today Carrie had on some skinny black leggings and a little pink off-the-shoulder T-shirt dress with a gold snakeskin belt that really showed off her tiny waist and big boobs. Carrie went down to Tanorife last night and was really tanned. She was more deep apricot colour than brown this time. Collette's new 'Girl from Mars' shade suited her a lot more than that 'Trinidad Girl', which is the one she's been getting done recently. Plus Carrie had loads of that Nars Body Glow she rubs on her shoulders, elbows and cleavage that gives her that 'movie star shimmer'. Carrie's makeup was done perfect too. She had on just a tiny touch of concealer 'cos she ain't got no spots at all, smoky kohl grey eyeshadow, loads of mascara, pink blusher and some golden honey-coloured lipgloss that made her lips look all wet. Her jewellery was quite plain – just solid gold hoops and her diamond necklace. She looked amazing.

I'm glad I didn't even try to compete. I just had on my navy Juicy hoodie and some jeans and white trainers, a bit of lip-gloss, that's that. '*Au naturelle*', as my Wes calls it, which is proper exotic for him. I think he must have learned it off an advert or something. Or maybe Sooz taught him it.

Bleugh. Sooz. Bleughghghghgh.

'Do I look OK?' Carrie asked, smoothing down her T-shirt.

'You look gorgeous,' I said, but I didn't want to go overboard with the praise. Her ego is well big already, sometimes, innit.

'What about the hair?' Carrie went on, pointing at her ponytail. 'What do you reckon?!'

And this is when I noticed Carrie's new Lithuanian hair extensions! Her ponytail was literally twice as thick and heavy as last time I was round her house to watch telly!

'Wow! That is well mental!' I said. I couldn't stop staring at it. I put my hand out and touched it and it freaked me out a bit to be honest. I was trying not to imagine where the hair had come from! See I watched a documentary about this the other week at Wesley's house when he was asleep. All that hair they use in extensions – well it comes from real people! I honestly don't think Carrie's worked this out, 'cos later on I saw her dangling some of the extensions in her mouth. OMG! I hope some old granny didn't die in that hair. I hope it ain't haunted! I worried about that for a little bit. This is why Wes says I shouldn't watch all those documentaries and stuff on Sky 'cos it just gives me stuff to worry about. Wes says that's why he watches stuff like *Crash Bang Bloodbath III* with Vin Diesel. 'Cos he don't want to think about anything. The last thing Wes needs, he says, after a long day mending people's toilets is to have to think about what's going on in the world. Maybe he's got a point.

'Right, then,' says Carrie, checking the train time table. 'There's a train in eight minutes. Let's do this shall we? Let's go and tell Genevieve Shaw that I am the next Supermodel Unmasked!'

'Yeah, fine', I said to her. 'But I'm just going to buy a can of Fanta for the journey.'

Well Carrie looked at her watch and tutted. 'We've not got time for that, Shiraz! We're running late you know?' Well usually I would have argued with her, but today I was feeling more Zen-like and calm, 'cos I'd been up since 6am listening to that *Whale Sounds* CD what I sometimes put on when Fin wakes up early wanting to be fed and I want to give Cava-Sue a lie in. That CD proper chills me out it does. A lot of folk in Essex could do with a listen of it.

Just then the train arrived in the station and me and Cazza ran down the stairs and jumped on it, and I must admit, it did feel a bit exciting all of a sudden. It felt like a proper adventure. I haven't felt like that for ages.

We got off the overground train at Stratford station in East London, where the Olympics site is, and then we got on the London Underground Jubilee Line which took us to North Greenwich where the O2 Arena is. We knew the way there easypeasy 'cos me and Caz went to the O2 once before last year to see a concert. Basically, this old bloke called Prince was playing there. He's a singer and he plays guitar. Me and Carrie hadn't really heard of him to be honest but Carrie's dad got some 'Hospitality Tickets', which meant we got to sit in one of the posh 'executive boxes', and have drinks and food, so we decided to go anyway. It was funny. It was a bit like being famous, 'cos we didn't have to sit squashed up with all the other thousands and thousands of normal folk. No, we had big squashy seats with a good view and a waitress to bring us drinks on a tray all lah-di-dah! Carrie was proper LOVING IT, 'cos all the people in the normal seats kept turning around to see who we were in the VIP boxes!! Carrie was getting well carried away and waving back at them. And one person even shouted to us, 'Who are you?' and Carrie just batted her eyelashes as if to say, 'Oh please don't make a fuss! I'm just a celebrity trying to have a normal night out!'

It was like she'd got lost in this fantasy world where she was a proper VIP, when in fact we'd got the tickets last minute for nothing 'cos her dad fitted some rich bloke's jacuzzi. Carrie loves all that type of thing though. People fussing around her. I don't. I found people staring at us a little bit embarrassing to be honest. I'm more about keeping it real. I'm just Shiraz Bailey Wood. I don't really want to be no one else. Take me or leave me. Me and Carrie were laughing about that night out when we were on the Jubilee Line.

' 'Ere what a racket that Prince geezer was, though eh, Shiz?' Carrie said to me.

'Man, he was well crap,' I agreed. 'He ain't got no tunes, innit?'

'None at all!' she said, 'I can't believe all those old fogeys were telling us he was a legend! They must be deaf or something. I was like, 'Oi, Prince bruv, play something we can dance to!'

'I know!' I said. 'There's no way he'd even make final eight on *X Factor*. Dunno how he sold millions of records?'

'Well, he was proper popular in the olden days,

weren't he?' said Carrie. 'And it's not like there was much else to do back then was there? I mean it must have been well boring and depressing, too, back when everything was black and white.'

Well I nearly wet myself laughing then.

'Carrie,' I said, 'Everything weren't black and white in the olden days! Just the *films* of the olden days are black and white! They hadn't invented colour films by then! The actual world was in colour, you total plant pot!'

'What do you mean?!' Carre said, getting out her new copy of *Heat* magazine which had a gorgeous picture of Tiffany Poole with long black hair wearing a ball gown covered in diamonds on the cover, exclusively revealing that one day she might adopt a baby from Africa.

'Oh nothing,' I said. Carrie was just winding me up about the black and white thing obviously. I hope she was winding me up anyway.

Soon afterwards we arrived at Greenwich North. The moment we got on to the proper hectic undeground platform I looked around me and noticed something really weird. The platform was completely full of girls, not one single boy at all, and nearly everyone was really tall! About five foot eleven. Some were six feet tall. Some were even bigger. I'm not being funny, but a LOT of these girls probably played the tree in the school play. And OK, I'm saying this 'cos I am jealous, 'cos I felt like a right gnome stood beside these girls, 'cos I'm only five foot four and Murph calls me 'MoonMask Poisondwarf' sometimes.

All these girls had to be the other *Supermodel Unmasked* girls arriving to audition! I could see Carrie starting to look quite nervous 'cos some of these girls were proper pretty, even if a lot of them weren't glamorous at all. No makeup, dressed all drab in just grey leggings or old jeans with no jewellery or nothing, like Carrie would only dress if she was in the house with a contagious illness that meant no visitors.

I gotta say, though, as I looked about the platform and looked at all the hundreds of faces, none of them in my opinion were as beautiful as Carrie Draper. And I'm not being fake or nothing here just because she's my friend. It's well depressing going anywhere with Carrie 'cos men in vans toot their car horns at her and wolf whstle all the time. None of these girls would get that type of attention I reckon 'cos a lot of them looked proper unapproachable and snotty.

Anyway, me and Carrie got on the really steep escalator and when we reached the fresh air and daylight, we both nearly fainted 'cos outside the O2 Arena there were thousands more girls! Most of them were in a big, wide long queue, wooshing out of the main doors of the arena and curving right round the side.

'Oh my God, it's twelve noon now! The judges go home at 5pm! I knew we should have set off earlier, Shiz,' Carrie tutted, looking at the silver Cartier watch that her mum and dad got her as a Confirmation pressie. She only wears it on special occasions, 'cos it was so expensive. I

64

just bit my lip and said nothing. To be honest, I'd given up any chance of meeting Genevieve Shaw now too.

So we joined the back of the queue and stood there for a long time. It moved forwards a few steps at one point, nothing much to get excited about. It weren't as if there was much of a happy atmosphere either. It were nothing like that time in Year Eleven, when tickets went on sale for McFly at Romford Ice Arena and me and Carrie and Chantalle Strong queued up for six hours. OH MY DAYZ! That time the queue was more fun than the actual gig 'cos everyone was singing and laughing and acting well daft. We met all sorts of nutters that day and people brought flasks of soup and bottles of wine and it was hilarious. Compared to that, the *Supermodel Unmasked* queue was sort of boring. At one stage a girl in front of us got out a tupperware box of salad and asked people if they wanted a forkful. One girl asked her if the salad dressing had oil in it, and another girl asked if there was any salad with the dressing on the side 'cos she didn't eat fat, and then everyone said no anyway. To be quite frank it was six hours since I'd had my Aldi Chocobangbangs and I could have eaten the salad plus the tupperware box, PLUS the scrawny hand of the girl that was holding it. Where are the magical Golden Arches of Maccy D's when you need them, eh?

So then Carrie pulled out her copy of *Heat* again and we both shared it and read about Tiffany Poole. Tiffany has been in the newspapers all week and on *GMTV* and

This Morning and folk have been talking about her on the radio, 'cos basically she said in an interview that she has so much to give emotionally and financially that she feels it's only fair to adopt an orphan at some point. Tiffany wants to bring the baby to London to live with her other kids in her mansion in Godalming in Surrey, so that he or she can share in the fruits of her sucessful designer bikini range, bestselling novel series and the profits from her new Astanga yoga DVD, *Get Thin – Stay Thin with Tiffany Poole*, which is out this month.

'I like to stay busy,' Tiffany Poole was saying, 'But the bottom line for me is family.'

'Oh my gosh, I love Tiffany Poole,' Carrie said to me. 'She's like a proper role model. I'm going to buy that new DVD she's bringing out. If it worked for Tiffany I'll give it a go. She's gone down from a size six to a size zero just by doing half an hour of standing about in a leotard and two of her Tiffany Poole Wellness Pills! No diet or nothing! In fact, it says here, Shiraz, that she eats chips all the time! And Steak and Kidney Pukka Pies! She just eats like a normal person. The pills zap the fat from your body, like magnets!'

'Carrie,' I said. 'You don't need to lose any weight. 'You're a size bloody ten. Size ten is tiny. I ain't been a size ten since I was in about Year Seven. Shut up.'

'Yeah, but my hips have got fat on them,' said Carrie not really listening. 'They're wide compared to my waist.'

'Oh, gngngngn.' I sighed, looking at her standing

there looking all perfect and curvy-shaped, like women are supposed to.

Just then the queue started moving a bit quicker. A big unfriendly woman who was about thirty-five and had a really false smile, and a clipboard, and was wearing a headset, was walking along the line talking to the girls. Some girls were getting told to go home then and there, and they were sobbing and making a fuss! Others were being pulled out and given red wristbands and being sent to the front of the queue. Me and Carrie stared at the lady proper hopefully as she got closer.

Suddenly, she stopped about ten metres in front of us and pointed at a weird girl who was wearing this beret with tinsel on it. Proper odd she was. I'd noticed her earlier on as everyone had been trying to move away from her in the queue 'cos she'd been muttering to herself. I felt a bit sorry for her. I don't reckon her head was in a good place. Now here she was being chatted to by the producer woman and given a wristband. Something seemed a bit fishy. I mean, fair enough the producer was definitely giving wristbands to the tallest skinniest girls who'd probably look nice with a bit of slap on, but some of the girls she was picking out ... well, I'm not being nasty or nothing, but honest to God, NO CHANCE! Yeah, I know that sounds shallow but I'm just keeping it real! There were girls getting red wristbands who were about five foot two with split ends and spots who'd obviously just got talked into coming down by their mothers, who no doubt reckoned they were gorgeous.

When the woman got level with us, she looked Carrie up and down well thoroughly and sort of chuckled a bit. Then she put her hand out and touched Carrie's pony tail and peered at it a bit and said, 'And where have you travelled from today?'

'I'm from Essex,' Carrie said.

Well the woman sort of giggled at the word 'Essex' like it was funny and to be honest I felt like kicking her to the curb then, 'cos that's my endz she was disrespecting and that ain't on, END OF STORY!

But then I remembered what me and my mate Uma Brunton-Fletcher agreed a long time ago, which is that violence is NEVER EVER the best policy when someone is stressing you out. NEVER. No, the best thing to do is take a deep breath and inside your head count slowly from one through to ten. Oh, and put a curse on them like a pikey would, 'cos pikey curses are strong and last for ever.

'I curse you, big wobbly *Supermodel Unmasked* woman,' I thought to myself. 'I hope the flaps of your ladygarden seal up and you have to wee through your ears forever.'

Then I smirked to myself 'cos she was proper oblivious to what I was thinking.

'OK, Carrie the Essex girl,' the producer said, pointing through the glass doors at the front of the queue. 'Take this wristband. You're through to the next round. Please move to Stage Two.'

'OH MY GOD, AMAZING!' squeaked Carrie, skipping away leaving me traipsing behind like her personal assistant, carrying her coat and her bag and bottle of Evian water and her copy of *Heat*. I looked back at the producer and I felt a bit tense.

So we both joined the queue for Stage Two. It was a lot shorter than the first one. Carrie's eyes were all wide like saucers and her hands were shaking. Stage Two wasn't so boring 'cos there was a film crew walking up and down filming it. There was a camera man, a sound guy with a big fuzzy thing on a stick to catch sound on, plus another production person asking questions. They were taking girls aside one by one and filming them against a big wall with *Supermodel Unmasked* posters all over it, chatting and being silly for the camera.

'They're filming stuff for the first episodes where you get to see all the auditions!' Carrie was saying. 'Oh my God, I could end up on Episode One! That's always one of the highest rated episodes! This is where it starts, Shiz! Oh my God!'

I just smiled and nodded.

Soon after that the film crew grabbed Carrie and made her talk about where her hoops and diamond necklace was from. Then they asked if she could say, 'I'm Carrie Draper! I'm an Essex girl! Watch out Gisele Bündchen! I'm the next Supermodel Unmasked!' Then they asked her to jump up and down doing rave dancing. I felt a bit weird when she did that, 'cos Carrie would never really say that or dance like that. But the camera men asked her to do it, so she just did. They asked her to do it about five times to work out what dance was the funniest.

Finally after about half an hour of waiting and being filmed, me and Carrie reached the front of the queue and were led into a little room where three women wearing headsets were sat behind a white plastic table. They didn't say hello, they just looked at Carrie, squinted a bit, then looked at their notes and one said quietly to the other two: 'Ha, perfect, just what episode one needs if you ask me.'

'Carrie the Essex Girl?' the woman in the middle said, as someone passed her a laptop with a video on it of Carrie doing starjumps and rave dancing, looking like a bit of a prat to be honest.

'That's me!' said Carrie, proper excited.

The three women stared at the laptop, then stared at Carrie, then muttered to each other a bit.

'Right, OK we're going to put you through to the next round,' she said. 'What that means is we're going to film you going before Genevieve Shaw and the judges. If they think you have model potential then this means you're down to the final twenty in the London pre-heats. If that happens, you come back tomorrow where we'll take twenty girls down to three. Then the final three from London go up against all the final threes from other cities and we still have eight more cities to go. Then there's twenty-four finalists and we condense them down to ten, and those ten will live in the model house. Do you understand all that?!'

'Erm, yeah, OK!' said Carrie.

I stood there in the background with my armfuls of bags and coats trying to work out what was going on. It was well freaky. Carrie was still a long way from living in the supermodel mansion but she'd actually done better than thousands of other girls today.

She looked so happy too!

Just then, another little film crew swarmed all around us and stuck their cameras in Carrie's face and asked her how she felt right now.

At the same time, a girl passed Carrie a piece of paper and said, 'Could you sign this legal consent form quickly please?'

'Right, OK,' said Carrie, taking the pen and the paper off her.

'Excuse me, what's that?!' I said. 'What do you want her to sign?

'Oh, it's just a piece of paper for our records!' said the girl, looking like I was being a bit of a nuisance.

I grabbed the piece of paper off Carrie and read it quickly. It was covered in all sorts of legal words that I couldn't understand, but there were a few lines in thick black type that I could work out, which said basically that Carrie was giving permission for everything *Supermodel Unmasked* filmed today to be shown on UK television FOREVER, and in every other country in the world, and on the internet and also on other planets and planets they'd not even discovered yet. Oh, and that Carrie had no rights over editing the footage or any right to sue anyone over how she looked and would earn no money from it at all 'cos they owned all the rights.

'Don't sign it Carrie!!' a little voice in my head said. It was the same little voice that told me not to let Wesley drive off that night in London after we snogged and before I let him go back to Sooz. The same little voice that told me not to stay in Ibiza with Carrie at the end of our holiday this summer. I ignored what my head was saying both of those times too.

'Everyone signs the form,' the researcher said. 'It's just a formality. If she doesn't sign it we can't film her so she can't proceed any further today.'

Carrie just looked at me like I was being silly and grabbed the paper out of my hands and squiggled her name in a big scrawl in the box, then we went through the doors to meet the judges.

Proper fast, with no time to think, a woman producer grabbed Carrie and got this weird microphone pack, like they wear all the time on *Big Brother* and pushed one bit up her T-shirt dress and clipped the speaking part to her collar and the box part of it to the back of her frock.

'Right, go,' she said, and pointed through the doors. Then she looked at me and rolled her eyes a bit and said, 'OK, you too, but hide at the back and be quiet.' Well I didn't like her tone of voice one little bit but there weren't no time for any more of my pikey frontbottom curses 'cos Carrie was already gone.

So I ran through the doors and at the end of the room was a long wooden table with three people sitting behind it staring ahead. The middle person was Genevieve Shaw! THE Genevieve Shaw off the telly! Sitting there looking all frosty, just like she always does on *Supermodel Unmasked*. In real life she is really really bone-thin, like a skeleton, and her head has this weird sort of plasticky look to it. I know I sound mean, but Genevieve Shaw ain't a nice person and she deserves it. In fact she deserves someone to say this to her face and film it and put it on telly. I reckon she might have had a load of that Botox stuff that Maria Draper sometimes gets injected into her face to make her look younger. That stuff actually freezes your face, it does! That's why no one knows for sure whether Maria Draper is happy or sad unless she proper specifically says, 'I am happy today' or, 'I am sad today'. It's all stupid if you ask me. My mother doesn't have any of this gubbins done and she wears ASDA cardigans and lets her hair go grey and I know she's not all glamorous like Maria, but I reckon she still looks better than the likes of Maria Draper 'cos at least she looks real. Keeping it real is important I think.

'OK, Carrie the Essex girl,' shouted Genevieve. 'Come on, let's take a look at you.'

So Carrie walked forward in front of the judges and they all peered at her for a bit and were totally silent. On the right of Genevieve was some skinny bird with short peroxide hair, wearing big dark sunglasses, who was the editor of a fashion magazine. And on the left was this ridiculous-looking tiny bloke in red lipstick and a wonky hat. He looked like a right twonk. François he was called. Apparently he is a 'legendary stylist to the stars'. Well he wanted to re-style himself, 'cos frankly he looked like a right doughnut.

'So, you think you're the next Supermodel Unmasked do you?' Genevieve said in her horrible voice, which sounds like an angry crow.

'Erm, yeah,' Carrie almost whispered. I don't think I've seen her look so frightened.

'And why's that?' said Genevieve, staring at her blankly.

'Erm, 'cos people say I'm pretty and stuff. And I . . .'

Well, all the judges started laughing at once then. Not in a nice way either.

'Oh well, call off the search then,' sighed Ratface in the hat.

'Oh, Suzie!' Genevieve said to Carrie, shaking her head slowly. 'This isn't about being pretty, it's about being a supermodel!'

'CUT!' yelled a man with headphones on, I think he was the sound man or the producer, or something. 'Genevieve, you called her Suzie, the girl is called Carrie.'

'Eh? Oh, Jeez. Can't we just go with Suzie?' tutted Genevieve.

'But my name is Carrie!' said Carrie, her lip was defo going a bit wobbly now.

'No, sorry. We'll need to re-record with the correct name for continuity,' said the soundman. 'Oh, and François,' he said to the prat in the hat, 'we'll pick up from your, "Call off the search" comment, which was absolutely great. But could you say it with a bit more sarcasm, this time? And everyone else on the panel, could you snigger a bit at it?'

'No problem,' they all said, looking quite bored. Carrie looked proper horrified. She opened her mouth to say something and then the director shouted, 'OK and . . . ACTION!'

Immediately, François in the hat looked at Carrie and curled up his face and said, 'Hah! Oh, you think you're pretty! Well CALL OFF THE SEARCH! Whoopie doo!' This time he did it proper sighing and clicking his fingers too. And the judges all laughed like it was the best joke anyone had ever heard in the world history of jokes since records began. My blood was starting to boil.

'OK, Carrie, let's see you walk! WALK WALK WALK!' shouted Genevieve, doing her famous catchphrase, waving her arms about like a bloody disco-dancing octopus. Genevieve's lips are all big and puffed out like a duckbilled platypus! In fact they look like she'd maybe threw up her dinner in an airplane toilet one time and the suction sucked her head in.

Carrie jumped a bit in shock as Genevieve shouted,

then she started to walk up and down like a catwalk model. Just like I've watched her practise in her bedroom and in the school yard since Year Seven. She always was the best in our class at it. All us girls were jealous sick of her.

'RIGHT, STOP WALKING! STOP WALKING!' shouted Genevieve, turning her head slightly to the side to look at Carrie, then frowning a bit. 'What's wrong with your knee?' 'Did you have an accident when you were a kid? Did a horse throw you off?'

'What do you mean?' Carrie said.

'It turns inwards when you walk. It affects your entire posture. You walk lopsided. It makes your whole face seem lopsided. Hang on. Unless your face IS lopsided? Actually I think it might be your face. Whatever, you're no use to me. It's a no from me. Designers won't hire a lopsided girl to show their clothes. I know this business, I've been in it twenty-five years!'

This woman was talking bloody rubbish. There is nothing lopsided about Carrie's knee or her face. If there was, you'd think I might have noticed. I've known her for fifteen years! Next to chip in was François, stylist to the stars.

'Ha! Well it was a no from me from the moment you walked in,' he said. 'Too average, too "girl next door", not tall enough, not great skin. Oh and too much boobs and ass for me. You're not my cup of tea, darling. You could do glamour modelling I'm sure. If that floats your boat.'

'Glamour modelling'???!! He meant *FHM* and *Nuts* and all that! Flaming cheek.

'OK, what François is trying to say,' said the girl in the dark glasses, who was at least trying to be slightly pleasant, 'is that you're a little on the large side for this kind of modelling. Size ten is slim in the real world but this is different, you'd be one of the biggest girls in the competition. Your boobs and bum wouldn't fit into the dresses. Maybe if you drop a stone or two, but to be blunt your face isn't editorial enough. I'm sure you're very pretty in Essex or wherever you're from, but you just haven't got the look. I'm sorry but that's a no from me. Thanks for coming.'

Well, Carrie just stood there, gobsmacked. She tried to walk away but her feet didn't seem to be working so she stood still again.

'Oh, incidentally,' Genevieve added, being totally serious. 'I can give you the number of a good surgeon who could look at your face if you want? Maybe you just need to reset your jaw and move your right ear downwards an inch?' Well at that point, I just bloody exploded. Carrie was properly crying now, so I ran forward to hug her and the director told me to get out of the bloody shot as they were still filming, and honest to God I just lost control of myself and I turned around and called him possibly the rudest word that I know – which I'm not proud of – and then I unclipped the microphone and chucked it into the hands of one of their gremlins and I picked up all the bags and coats and dragged Carrie outside.

It was only then that I properly sussed that they'd been filming Carrie from Essex for something funny to fill up episode one, along with the small fat girl with spots, and the slightly mad girl in the tinsel beret. Carrie would be the Essex girl who reckoned she could be a supermodel. HA BLOODY HA.

We walked in silence out of the doors of the O2 Arena, back past the queue, which was even longer than when we'd arrived and was full of excited-looking young girls. I wanted to shout at them, 'Honest bruv, don't bother!' but I knew I'd just look like an idiot, like one of them loonies on *The X Factor* who start causing a big fuss when their friend don't get through and start shouting at Simon Cowell, and security gets called to remove them. I wasn't giving the *Supermodel Unmasked* people anything more to laugh at.

'Right, I know where we're going,' I said to Carrie, pointing at a sign on a wall that always brings joy to my heart. It had a pair of magical holy golden arches on it and the message: 'McDonalds 800 METRES – turn left'. Me and Caz walked slowly, following the red arrows on the pavement, my arm linking though her skinny little arm. At one point she started crying again so I gave her a hug and plonked a kiss on her bony cheekbone and said, 'Come on. They must be giving out the Parrot Fandango drums by now. I'm getting us both one.'

Once we'd sat down with our Happy Meals and our amazing toy drums, I looked Carrie proper square in the eye and I said, 'Look, Caz I'm going to say something now and I want you to take it in, right? Proper listen to me, eh? And even if you don't take it in now, I want it to register somewhere in your head and make sense sometime very soon, when your head's in less of a spin. OK?'

'Yeah,' sighed Carrie, looking inside her Happy Meal box and pulling out her fries and just staring at them.

'Your face is NOT lopsided,' I said, 'And your knee does NOT turn inwards. And you're NOT fat! In fact you're skinny. Everyone says you're skinny! You're a size ten Carrie. Size ten is thin. You could do with putting weight on! And you're NOT average looking! You were the bloody prettiest girl at Mayflower Academy Carrie! It used to drive the older girls mental! Remember when we were in Year Seven and those nightmare rudegirls in Year Eleven started proper giving us evils every day and threatening to stab us? You know why that was? 'Cos even aged eleven you were the prettiest girl at Mayflower. That's a fact. I just don't hardly say this 'cos I don't want you going all big-headed on me! But it's true Caz!'

Carrie smiled a little bit then, but not much, and then her face went back to looking sad, like she was replaying what those pig judges had said to her all over again.

'It's all pantomime, Caz! It ain't nothing personal,' I said, 'cos that's what Davina off of *Big Brother* always says to the housemates when they come out of the *Big Brother* house and people are shouting abuse and being proper nasty. But the moment I said it I realised for the first time it didn't really make no sense. The fact is, if someone is making personal remarks about you and how you walk and how you look, how can it NOT be personal?! I wished I could drag that François bloke down to McDonalds now so that he could see what he'd done to my best friend and say sorry. Oh who was I kidding, François would never come to McDonalds. I bet he don't even know what a McDonalds is. He probably has fancy-schmancy calorie-controlled meals delivered to his house by courier three times a day, like all those famous celebrities in *Heat* do, 'cos they're too bloody lazy to do their own shopping. Oh it made me so mad!

I got my Parrot Fandango drum out of its plastic bag and gave it a bit of a bang to let off steam. The staff serving behind the counter gave me the evil eye. It was almost as if they'd got a bit sick of hearing customers banging the drums in the restaurants when they were working ten-hour shifts for minimum wage and hated us and wanted us to go. But I was on a mission to cheer Carrie up so I banged it a bit more and soon, after a bit of prodding and a lot of silly jokes, I got Carrie laughing and then I got her banging her drum and singing with me, 'Goodmayes Girl Run Ting! Goodmayes Girl Run Ting! La la la!' And pretty soon after that we got chucked out of McDonalds by a bloke with five stars on his lapel who was clearly a hater of decent tuneage.

'Shiz,' Carrie said to me when we got outside. 'Do you mind if we do something before we go home? Can we go up West? Can we just hop on the tube now and go down to Oxford Street? It's just I put my name down for this bloody audition thing and I don't want to go and I know I won't get it or nothing but the woman was nice and she fitted me in at the end of the day especially. I'd feel crap for not showing up. Oh, and the office is beside Top Shop. We can go there afterwards. I need new earrings anyway.'

'Oh OK,' I laughed. 'What is it? It's not another modelling show please God though, is it?'

'Nah,' sighed Carrie almost cringing at the thought, 'The woman just said they needed bright people for a TV show what's going to be on Saturday nights on BBC1 before *The National Lottery*. It's like a quiz or something. General knowledge. Oh I dunno, I weren't listening properly. It seemed a good idea at the time but that last audition was so horrible I can hardly face it. But my dad's giving me loads of hassle about finding a job, so I made all these appointments to prove to him I was being busy and, oh God Shiz, I dunno . . .' Carrie's voice sort of trailed off then and her face went sad again.

'Come on then, Cazza,' I said, 'It won't hurt to pop by.'

But, dear God in heaven! Carrie Draper on a quiz? I kept my face totally normal like this was perfectly reasonable. At least she wasn't sobbing her heart out any more.

We got to the offices of Star TV International at about 5.45pm as they were just about locking the doors.

'Ah, Carrie Draper! I spoke to you yesterday! You're here to apply for *Brainbox Bloodbath*?!' a smiley woman with a clipboard said when we arrived. 'And are you applying too?' she said, pointing at me.

'Erm, what is the show exactly?' I said, trying to keep a straight face. Oh come on, Shiraz? *BRAINBOX BLOODBATH*! Oh my days!!

'Well the clue is in the title!' the woman said. 'It's a general knowledge quiz for eighteen-to-thirty-year-olds, where you pit your wits against other brainboxes! Then if you get through to the final Battle Round at the end of every show, you change into lycra costumes and crash helmets and go head-to-head with your rival, standing on towers ten metres above the ground. You have to whack each other about the head and body with those giant cotton buds things like on *Gladiators* until one of you falls off! Whoever stays on is the winner!'

I kicked Carrie's ankle a bit and we both started giggling. Then I tried to stop myself but this made the next giggles come out like proper snorty pig ones. The woman looked at us both and sighed.

'Oh, don't worry, no one gets hurt!' she said. 'It isn't actually a bloodbath! I mean yes, someone got a broken nose and a detached retina the other day when we were testing the equipment. But our technical department are going to redesign the crash helmets! It's going to be great!'

'Hahahhahahhahah!' I said, starting to laugh properly now. I just couldn't help myself.

'Oh, amazing! I'm glad you like the sound of it!' said the woman, pushing forms in our hands, 'Now all you need to do today is take this simple general knowledge quiz and hand it back to me. You've got twenty minutes – good luck!'

Me and Carrie sort of tumbled through into the room where we had to take the tests, giggling. Then Carrie looked at the paper. Laughed a bit again and whispered,

'Oh God, Shiraz, no way! Listen to this? 'Who wrote *The Tennant of Wildfell Hall*? Oh who bloody cares? I'm going to write Beyoncé Knowles. B-E-Y-O-N-C-E K-N-O-W-L-E-S! There, that's question one done. 'Ere, what time do you reckon Top Shop closes? Is Thursday late-night shopping?' I just giggled again and looked at the quiz.

'Anne Bronte,' I wrote down for question one. That was easy to be honest. I read that book in Year Twelve just after me and Joshua Fallow split up. It was OK. I finished it, but only 'cos I was waiting three hundred and forty-seven pages for the actual exciting plot to start up, like it does in *Jane Eyre*, which is by Anne's sister, Emily Bronte. Well I got mugged off big time 'cos it never really did. It was just a load of posh folk in the countryside wanting to get off with each other but never quite managing it. That's what them books by Jane Austen are like too. I read three of them waiting for something juicy to happen and, honest bruv, NO JOY.

I looked down the rest of the question list, the others seemed quite easy too. There was one about dinosaurs and one about Joan of Arc and one about the rainforests and one about Shakespeare and one about Condoleeza Rice that American politician. Just stuff I sort of knew anyway. Well I think I knew it. Answers just sprung into my head so I scribbled them down. Oh, God, what am I saying, they were probably all wrong.

After about fifteen minutes, me and Carrie handed back the forms and gathered up our stuff and started to leave the office. But just as we got halfway down the stairs, the researcher woman came out of the office and shouted after us, 'Hang on! Shiraz Bailey Wood? Which one are you?'

'That's me,' I said, turning round.

'Can I have a quick word?' she said.

I walked back up the stairs. The woman looked proper buzzing off her head.

'Listen, I've just checked your paper very quickly and I can tell you that you've been one of our highest scorers today! We made those questions really difficult, you know? You've done amazingly well!'

'Really?' I said. I wasn't giving her the pleasure of seeing me look all happy, 'cos I knew what she was up to.

I'd got a rubbish score and they wanted to film me making a prat of myself.

'Yes, really!' she said. 'Look, I can give you a wristband to get you to the next round now, if you like? If you pass that round you're seriously close to being one of the contestants on series one of *Brainbox Bloodbath*!'

'Honest?' I said. I was quite sarcastic this time 'cos I wanted her to know that she wasn't getting one over on me, even if I was some silly cow from Essex.

'Honest!' she said, 'You were the only person in two days who knew that Joan of Arc was executed at the age of nineteen.'

I looked at her and gave her my best Shiraz Bailey Wood dead-eye expression.

'Yeah, bare jokes bruv. JOG ON,' I said, and I walked down the stairs and out of the door with my head held high and all of my pride still intact. Then me and Carrie went on to Top Shop and looked at the earrings and didn't say no more about it.

Yeah, course I was one of the cleverest people that auditioned.

They must have took me for a RIGHT IDIOT.

NOVEMBER

FRIDAY 11TH NOVEMBER

I was happy when Carrie called me this morning 'cos she's been a bit quiet of late. I reckon all that *Supermodel Unmasked* business did her head in a bit. It was bound to though, weren't it? I phoned Carrie up last Wednesday after I'd got paid by Collette and Cava-Sue and asked her if she wanted to go down Vue with me and watch that new movie, *Love You To Death* with Vanessa Hudgen. They've been banging on about it all week on *GMTV* and on Virgin radio. It's about this girl who's a bikini model but also a serial killer. It ain't really my type of thing but Caz loves stuff like this. I love eating the big box of jelly snails and flying saucers and cola cubes we always buy. And getting a hot dog covered in mustard and ketchup and watching trailers for other movies that are coming. 'Cos whenever one looks really really boring, like it's a Norwegian film with subtitles about suicide, I always say to Caz in a proper excited voice, 'Don't look Carrie, it'll spoil the surprise!' Then I put my hand over her eyes and she always laughs her head off.

Well, anyway, Carrie didn't want to go down the Vue last Wednesday. Carrie said she was going to Fitness First gym instead, to take an extra spinning class called

Extreme Bootie Blitz, 'cos she is working on shaping her bum as it's going a bit flabby. So I says to Carrie, OK, but did she fancy getting a takeaway from Spirit of Siam any time that weekend and just watching some telly together. But Carrie said she weren't eating takeaways any more 'cos that's why she was gaining all the weight. All that monosodium glutamate stuff they put in the Chinese food was going straight to her bottom and giving her cellulite!

I just sighed when she said that, 'cos Carrie hasn't got cellulite.

' 'Ere Caz,' I said. 'Have I done something to offend you? Are you avoiding me or something?

'Don't be daft, Shizza, I'm telling the truth. I'm just on a health kick right now!' Carrie said. 'It's a bit like when Angelina Jolie goes into training for a Hollywood movie and gets all buff and does boot camps and stuff. I'm getting into training to be famous!'

Well I sort of laughed when she said that, but later when I thought about it, it made me feel sad. I like the Carrie I've got right now, even though she is proper insane in the brain and gets me into trouble all the bloody time. I mean, I was reading all my old diaries the other night and proper cringing at what we've got up to. I don't want her to change. And what's the point in life if you can't have a nice box of jelly snails and some Singapore spicy noodles and a bag of prawn crackers now and again?

So anyway, this morning at about 7 am, I was down in the kitchen cuddling Fin while Cava-Sue was getting her shower when my phone bleeped with a text. It was Carrie. Well this made no sense 'cos Carrie ain't ever up at 7 am? The only explanation seemed to be that Draperville had burned down in the middle of the night and Cazza was stood outside in her La Senza teddy staring at the charred ruins, needing somewhere to live. OK, I'm being sarcastic here, but safe to say, Carrie don't do early mornings. She is well lazy. In fact a few years ago she slept right through the Goodmayes tornado that was on the BBC news and everything, which uprooted all the trees in her mother's Japanese style garden and totally destroyed the authentic plywood Japanese Hacienda that Barney had just had delivered from B & Q.

Carrie missed all of this. She was out-cold snoring!

I picked up my phone and shook my head in disbelief.

'U up by any chance Shizzle? XX' the text read.

I got her number on speed dial and stuck the phone in the crook of my neck 'cos I was holding a baby. Obviously, our Fin started grabbing at the phone right away 'cos he is well obsessed with phones and tries to eat every one he sees. We reckon when Fin grows up he'll either work for T-Mobile or he'll be a mugger. I hope it's the first one.

So the phone's ringing and I've got a small person swatting at my ear and toast beginning to burn and then Carrie picked up and said, 'Oh my dayz! Did I wake you up?!'

'No! I was up anyway,' I said, 'I'm always up early. We've got a baby living here, we've got no choice. What are you doing awake, Carrie Draper?'

'I'm excited!' she says to me. 'And you're going to be too! What you doing today?!'

'Erm, nothing much,' I said. 'Wes is off work 'cos he's had a job cancelled last minute. Wes says I should go over to his and watch a DVD . . . hang on why?'

'Brilliant! And what is Penny doing?!' said Carrie.

'Penny?' I said. 'My Penny, the Staffy?'

'Yeah, Penny the wonderdog!' she said.

'Erm well let's have a look,' I said taking the cordless phone into the hallway with Fin in one arm and looking in Penny's basket. 'Well, I'm not gonna lie to to you, Caz, she ain't looking very lively. She's on her back with her feet all up in the air. Oh and she's dreaming about something 'cos her snout is moving and her paws are flicking about. Oh my gosh! And she's got Tiq's Macca Pacca doll from *In The Night Garden* in there with her and it's covered in dog drool. Oh bloody hell, Pen! You ain't meant to have that. I'm gonna have to stick it in the wash now. Bad dog!'

'Excellent!' laughed Carrie. 'This is just what I want to hear! So, do you fancy going down Bluewater today? They're only doing auditions for *Doggy Detention* down there today! *DOGGY DETENTION*!!! *Doggy* bloody *Detention*! You know the show I mean?'

'Yeah, 'course I do, everyone watches it! Weren't it

like the highest rated show on BBC1 this year?' I laughed, 'It's the one where they take dogs that are proper spoilt brats and they make them go back to dog school and get all their faults seen to by the best dog trainers in Britain! And the lessons are in that old creepy Victorian boarding school covered in cobwebs and the owners have to live in the school for a week with the dogs and wear school uniform!'

'That's it! That's the one! I never really understood the school uniform part. That don't seem to have any point to it though does it?' Carrie said.

'Yeah, that is a bit random that bit, innit?' I said. 'Anyway, what do you want to do? Do you wanna go down Bluewater and watch the auditions!?'

'No, Shizza,' she said excitedly. 'I want us to go down with your Penny and my Alexis and AUDITION OURSELVES! Oh come on! I think I'd be perfect! I mean, both of us, we'd both be perfect! Do you reckon your Wes would drive us in his Golf?' Ring Wes now! Go on! Please!'

Well, she sounded so bloody excited about it I couldn't help but say yes. And I know I'd said to myself no more reality TV show auditions after the *Supermodel Unmasked* fiasco, but the truth is I bloody love *Doggy Detention*. It's one thing that the whole Wood family watch together.

Well my Wes was a sweetheart when I rang him. He just laughed a bit and said, 'Oh all right. I'll get in the shower and come over.' And as I started getting ready I was thinking about what a one in a million boyfriend he is. He's proper chilled out is Wes and never really kicks off about Carrie and her daft plans that much. I mean he has a dig now and then but he sort of respects that she's my best mate and that best mates are important. And I was thinking about all this as I heard his banana-yellow Golf pull up outside and I looked out of the window and I realised Wes wasn't alone. He had his bloody best mate Bezzie Kelleher with him! Gngngnggngn! Now that's totally DIFFERENT. That weren't part of the plan at all!

Bezzie Kelleher don't make me feel very chilled out at all. Why did I make a big point of saying he don't get enough fresh air?! Now he's going to be breathing my air! And it wasn't as if he wasn't getting any fresh air then neither 'cos I could see him perfectly clearly sitting in the front seat sparking up a bloody joint and opening the window to let the fumes out! WHAT A FLAMING LIBERTY?!

I pulled my dressing gown on over my thong and bra 'cos I wasn't dressed yet and I stormed downstairs with my arms crossed wearing my Scotty dog slippers and banged on the car window. Bezzie jumped a bit and Wesley started laughing.

'Oi, bruv, do you wanna put that joint out? What do you think you're playing at smoking weed outside my yard? My mother could come past and smell that. Put it out now.'

Bezzie rolled his eyes a bit at me, but he stubbed the end out.

Meanwhile my Wes was giggling like mad. 'I told him he'd be in trouble, innit,' said Wes, laughing.

'Yeah, well, YOU should have stopped him! Kids play around here. Do you know how hard some of these mothers are working round here to keep their kids from smoking weed?! Hang on! Are you smoking too, Wesley?!'

'Course I ain't, innit!' Wesley said. 'You know I don't smoke! And anyway I'm driving. It's all him! Awww don't be all up in my face like a rudegirl, princess, innit!'

'Don't "princess" me, Wesley Barrington Bains II,' I said. 'And if there's so much as a joint's worth of grass in this car, well I ain't getting in, 'cos I'm not driving all the way to Bluewater all paranoid every time we see a bloody police car!'

'I ain't got no more, Shiz!' said Bezzie, 'I swear I ain't. I'm bloody skint.'

'Well, OK then,' I said, 'I'm going to trust you for now then Bezzie, but you'd better watch yourself bruv.' Then I smiled at Wesley. 'Right, have you had any breakfast yet by the way?'

'No,' they both said.

'Right, come inside and get some toast while I get my makeup on.'

So I got my hoodie on and my jeans and my gold hoops and some makeup and my new Nikes, then I gave our Penny's coat a bit of a brush to get the best of the carpet fluff and Pot Noodle soy sauce stains off her and I washed up all the breakfast dishes and then we tried to set off. By this point we were running quite late. We were supposed to be at Carrie's for ten-thirty, but by quarter to eleven we were still trying to lure Penny down the path outside the house and into Wesley's car. But Pen – who is proper brainy by the way, just like a police dog – had proper sussed there was something out of the ordinary going on and had started lying down and gripping her paws tight to the floor.

In the end I had to steal my mother's special box of Cadbury's Chocolate Fingers that she keeps in a special tin and which me and Murph and Cava-Sue ain't allowed to even touch or look at or we get killed to death, and I had to use them to bribe Penny. It worked out at one Chocolate Finger every two metres.

'This is going to be a well expensive day out if it goes on like this innit?' sighed Wesley.

'Yes, but this stubborness is something I'm hoping they'll be able to iron out in *Doggy Detention* Wesley!' I said. 'This just makes me more certain we're doing the right thing!'

'Why don't we just pick her up and shove her in the car?' said Bezzie. 'Will she bite me?'

' 'Course she don't bite,' I said to Bezzie. 'Try and pick her up if you want . . .'

So Bezzie walked up to Penny, limbering up like they do on that *World's Strongest Man* competition that's always on telly on bank holidays. Then he squats beside Penny and puts his arms gently round her chest and tail and tries to lift her. Well his eyes nearly popped out of his head.

'Oh my God, how fat is she!? It feels like she's made of cement. That ain't right! That is one fat dog!'

I narrowed my eyes at Bezzie Kelleher,

'Penny ain't fat! She's just big boned,' I said. 'You're worse than that bloody vet, you are! I reckon she might have emotional problems so she comfort-eats a bit. But that's fine 'cos I'm going to have this checked out today on *Doggy Detention*.'

By this point my Wesley had laid a trail of biscuits up to the car door and Penny was gobbling them up one by one until she finally jumped into the back seat. The car wobbled a bit when she got in, then we jumped in quickly and set off.

Our Penny didn't look very happy at first. She must have thought we were off to see the vet again. He's proper forward, he is. He pokes glass thermometers up her bum and shines torches in her eyes. Poor Penny started to whimper a bit like she was scared. I reckon she was remembering that time she ate an entire one of Murphy's socks and it went right through her digestive system and then twenty-four hours later, bits of wool started emerging from her rear end! We had to take her to the emergency vet, and he put his plastic gloves on and pulled the rest of it out with a big pair of tweezers and then charged us eighty quid! We never knew why Penny ate the sock. It was the stupidest thing she ever did. I opened the window of Wesley's car and let some air in and Penny started enjoying our journey to Bluewater a lot more. She stood with her paws on my knee and her face in the gap letting the air rush past her nose. This made her really happy.

We arrived at Draperville at quarter past eleven. I texted Caz to say we were outside and she came down to the electric gates carrying Alexis in a little pink handbag dog-carrying thing, with its wet nose and tufty ears poking out of the top. Alexis looked pretty stupid to be honest. The thing is Alexis IS pretty stupid. She's one of them dogs that you can't even go down the park and play fetch the ball with 'cos she finds the rules a bit over-complex. So basically, you chuck the tennis ball and Alexis runs and finds it then runs off in the opposite direction with it in her gob, then you spend the rest of the time chasing her.

Today, the silly fluffy gonk had on a denim jacket and a pink beret! It was doing its yap yap yap thing as it was carried along. Yap yap yap yap yap yap! The thing is, when Alexis yaps, Carrie talks back to it and that makes it yap even more! Carrie can stand for hours on end in the kitchen in Draperville going, 'Alexis! Say hello!' and Alexis yaps. Then Carrie goes, 'Good girl!' then Carrie says again, 'Alexis, say HELLLLO!' and the bloody thing yaps and Carrie goes, 'Good girl, Alexis!' And believe me Carrie and Alexis can play this game for HOURS and never get bored. And Alexis gets fed those proper expensive little silver foil trays of food that are about a quid each which come in flavours like Roast Duck with Chicken Liver Pate'. The ones that have got a picture on the packet of another really spoilt small yappy dog wearing a crown and sitting on a plump cushion. The spoilt little git.

And how does Alexis repay them? She wipes her bum on their carpets! She actually puts her bum onto the cream carpets, lifts up her little fluffy back legs and scurrys along on her front ones leaving a skidmark! The vet says it's 'cos sometimes dogs get worms and they get itchy bums! OH MY DAYS it is minging. (OK, minging but totally hilairous. Especially when Maria Draper sees the skidmark and stands there with her face that don't move 'cos it's full of Botox saying, 'Mrs Raziq, I am not very happy, there appears to be a poo stripe on my carpet! Could you please book Alexis in to see the vet? I think she might have worms again. And buy another litre bottle of 1001 Stain Vanish from Waitrose too please.'

Oh, and another of Alexis's tricks is to go into Carrie's bedroom and rob things and drag them downstairs. So one night recently Barney Draper was having a poker evening with all his mates and everything was all very tense 'cos they were playing for big money and all the men were drinking fine Scotch and being all blokesh and then suddenly the door to the lounge creaked open and in trots Alexis WITH A SANITARY TOWEL STUCK TO

HER HEAD! HAHAHAHAHAHA! She'd fished it out of Carrie's bin! Carrie won't even talk about that she's so mortified. Oh and the chief number one worst thing Alexis ever did was escape from Draperville one night and turn up three days later pregnant! And Carrie and her parents didn't even know until sixty-three days later when Alexis starts lying on her side near the ornamental pond puffing and panting and then little puppies began to appear! And honest to God these were the weirdest puppies you've ever seen. They were like half Chihuahua/half spotty Dalmatian! Black and white coats with spots, with blonde fluffy ears! I made a mental note of all this stuff to tell the TV researchers from *Doggy Detention* when we arrived.

I was shocked when I saw Carrie, to be honest, 'cos she looked thinner than usual. She looked like she'd lost a dress size. Maybe it was just 'cos she was dressed in black and had those new hair extensions. Her hair was so big it made her body look small? Or maybe her skin was so apricot-coloured it made her face look just that bit thinner? Or maybe the daft cow just wasn't bloody eating anything, and going down spinning classes all the time, and being a plank. I really hoped it wasn't the last one.

Carrie looked into the car as she walked towards us and spotted her ex-boyfriend Bezzie Kelleher. Her face was a bloody picture. She looked at me in the back seat, sitting with Penny on my knee nearly suffocating me and she mouthed, 'Shiraz!?'

Yeah, I knew she was going to have a go at me later about not warning her Bezzie was coming. But if I'd told her Bezzie was coming beforehand she'd have just had a massive go at me! And anyway, this weren't about us, it was about making our dogs better pets for the future wasn't it? Carrie needed to get over herself and realise that.

'Aight Bezzie, aight, Wes,' said Carrie when she got in, chewing gum and looking out of the window.

'Caz,' said Wesley, nodding.

'How's it going, Carrie?' said Bezzie, proper craning round to get a look at her, 'You look amazing, innit.'

'Ta,' she said, staring back at him. Bezzie had on his Roc-A-Wear hoodie. I remember him wearing it when we used to go down Dagenham to the Car Cruises almost three years ago. He had dark circles round his eyes from where he'd been up all night playing *Grand Theft Auto* on-line with people in America. Carrie didn't say that Bezzie looked 'amazing' back to him, and let's face it, it would have been a lie, but I kind of wish she had said something nice, just to be polite, 'cos it felt well awkward.

Anyway, we set off to Bluewater – four of us and two dogs all squashed in one car. Penny just stared at Alexis when she got in the car as if to say, 'Oh God, not you again,' and Alexis just looked a bit blank, 'cos let's face it, Alexis only has a teeny little brain, as light as a Kinder Bueno, so she wouldn't remember the other three-hundred-and-forty times she'd met Penny. Both dogs seemed to quite enjoy the journey anyway 'cos Alexis was yapping at every traffic light and Penny had her whole head out of the window barking at passing cars. And at one point a bus went past really close and Penny got a fright and did one of her extra-special guffs what just seep out silently and then when they reach your nose you feel like your eyes are melting. Then the fart took over the whole air supply of the entire car and everyone was choking and screaming. Still it broke the ice a bit 'cos we all had a laugh.

'That dog ain't well!' Bezzie was shouting. 'That's not a natural smell. That's what evil smells like. Like if you met Satan! He'd smell like that wouldn't he?' Penny looked proper pleased with herself when everyone was laughing. That's the thing about Penny, bless her. She spreads joy wherever she goes.

Soon we arrived at Bluewater and found a space to park and jumped out and gave the dogs some water. The car park was full of people with dogs on leads. There were Poodles, Alsatians, King Charles spaniels, red setters, Dalmatians, every type of dog you could think of. None were as beautiful or intelligent as my Penny, though. Or as stupid-looking as Alexis. I had a good feeling in my bones about this one. So did Carrie. We were on to a winner, we thought.

Wes and Bezzie went off to the Vue multiplex to watch *Car Killer VI*, that movie about a bloke with a car who is a killer and God knows how they've made five of them already 'cos the first one was proper gubbins. In fact I fell asleep in my jelly snails.

Meanwhile, me and Carrie started discussing our plan of action. We agreed to storm in there all guns blazing and wow those *Doggy Detention* people. OH MY GOSH this was really exciting!

We followed the signs which said **BBC:** *Doggy Detention* **Auditions** into a meeting centre underneath Bluewater. We were met by this nice friendly bloke with blonde hair called Aled who had a headset on and some proper extra extra low-slung jeans that meant we could see his underpants and their washing instructions and the top of his bum crack and everything. He was well smiley and chatty and he wrote mine and Carrie's names and our dogs names down and he filled in a few details about the things we wanted to 'iron out in our dogs' behaviour'. So I told him about the carpet poo stripes and the Cadbury's Chocolate Fingers and the guffs and he nearly widdled his grunderpants laughing. And then he says, 'So are you two good friends then?' pointing at me and Carrie.

'Yeah, we're best mates,' says Carrie. 'We've known each other for years.'

'I've been trying to get rid of her for years, more like,' I said. 'She's a stalker though. She keeps finding me.'

'The thing is,' Carrie jumped in. 'I met Shiraz when I was at nursery, everyone knew her 'cos she was the girl who took the top off the doll's house and did a poo in the bathroom area!'

Well everyone in the queue was laughing by now, and my face was going proper red!

'She's exaggerating, of course,' I said. 'But don't worry, I've got plenty of shameful stories to tell you about her!'

'You two make a good double act!' said Aled. 'Would you consider going on *Doggy Detention* as a couple. It would be visually funny too because you'd have this tiny little pretty dog and this big fat Staffy who looks quite tough.'

'Penny isn't fat though, she's just big boned,' I said, my eyes narrowing just a bit.

'Well quite,' Aled agreed. 'So . . . was that a yes then?'

'Yes!' me and Carrie both said. 'Yes of course!'

'OK then, here's a sticker,' Aled said, slapping one on both of our top halves. 'And the dogs both get red ribbons for their collars. Could you make your way through the double doors and go into the next stage?!'

We couldn't stop laughing as we went. On reflection, I should have realised then that Penny was starting to grow a bit bored with all this 'moving around being energetic' business. I mean let's be honest, Penny is only usually awake for about two hours a day. And the rest of the time she's on her back getting some solid gold kip action, pushing out zeds, dreaming of imaginary parks and imaginary cats while going precisely nowhere in a basket under the stairs. So by the time we'd reached the second interview, Penny was already lying flat on the floor refusing to budge. In fact I dragged her into the room to meet the next set of TV people. DRAGGED HER! I pulled her in on her lead behind me like a giant floor cleaner, attracting dust and old ciggie ends as she went. Talk about embarrassing. Luckily this next interview was mostly about me and Carrie not our dogs.

It was just like a chat to be honest. Basically, a couple of women filmed me and Caz with video-recorders talking about our friendship. It wasn't all freaky and fake like at *Supermodel Unmasked*. It's only when I sat down and talked to strangers about it that I properly realised how much me and Cazza have been through. We told them about the time we did the Mayflower Academy Winter Festival and the school hall burned down. And the time we fell out over Bezzie Kelleher. And all the times we've had arguments and made friends again and about the times we've been out raving. And about how we're basically like proper chalk and cheese in our personalities but how opposites attract 'cos we're still best mates after all these years. We sounded like an old married couple! I did most of the talking I think. I'm terrible once I get going. I'm like my nan, she can talk the leg off a shop dummy.

'You're very funny,' one of the ladies, Lizanne, said. 'I think you'd make great telly! I mean, both of you will. You're both very funny.'

'Thanks,' we both said, double-checking her expression to see if she was taking the mickey or not.

'I agree! I love your energy!' said the other woman, who was called Clarissa. 'Just out of chance, are you free around about Christmas? Early January time? Obviously we'd need to check out all sorts of other things before putting you on the show, but if all went well, how would you feel about being part of the new series? We're moving to BBC1 primetime so there would be a lot of exposure for you both!'

'Yes!' said Carrie, instantly. I just looked at them and felt a bit shocked. It was all happening so fast.

'Erm, well yeah, I suppose, I mean . . . yeah,' I said.

'You two would be like the Trinny and Susannah of *Doggy Detention*!' said Clarissa. 'You'd be famous overnight!'

'Wow!' said Carrie, her face was glowing, like someone had just flicked her ON switch at the back again.

'OK, well the next stage is,' said Lizanne, 'that we need to get some good footage of your dogs running and walking and really get to know their personalities! So why don't you both take a little breather outside then we'll grab some lunch and then it's on to stage three!'

'OK then!' Carrie said, picking up Alexis and putting her back inside her pink handbag thing. I stood up and rattled Penny's lead to tell her to move. But the thing was Penny didn't fancy moving. She didn't fancy 'a little breather'. She just lay there. So I tried to drag her out like I'd dragged her in but then she did her special annoying move of flipping over and lying flat on her back. And honestly it is proper impossible to drag Penny anywhere when she lies on her back. Penny knows this. She's done it before a few times in Goodmayes Park! The lead gets all tangled up in her paws and then she whimpers so it looks like she's suffering extreme animal cruelty and nosy-parkers start calling the RSPCA on their mobiles and filming the evidence. Eventually I threw the lead down on the floor to stop it getting tangled and watched Penny in proper dismay as she just lay on her back with her feet in the air and her eyes shut and her tongue lolloping out to the side pretending to be dead.

My face was starting to go really red! Because at first Clarrissa and Lizanne found it funny but then they started to get a bit annoyed 'cos we were cluttering up their meeting room and they had to move elsewhere to have their private discussion. Eventually one of them said, 'It could be a problem if the dog is this disruptive during filming!' Well then Carrie started to get a bit irate now too.

'Shiraz!' she hissed. 'Will you tell that dog of yours to behave itself! It's making a right show of us!'

'It's *Doggy* bloody *Detention*!' I snapped back at her. 'That's why Penny is here! What do you think she's gonna do? Jump through a burning hoop and catch a bone! You knew very well she had issues surrounding discipline when we brought her here! She's only keeping it real! She ain't being fake!'

'Well,' hissed back Carrie, 'can't she keep her issues on the downlow until we're at least past this next round!? Did you hear that woman, Shiraz? We could be the next Trinny and Susannah! I could be on the front of the *Radio Times*! Um, I mean we both could!'

Well at this point things started to go very very Pete Tong. 'Cos while we were arguing Penny had stood up 'cos something had got her attention. A smell of food had started wafting through the rooms. Next door the catering people had started serving some lunch to the *Doggy Detention* crew. Our Penny had got a right nose full of chicken curry and in a flash she was offski! Out of the room and off down the corridor. And me and Carrie didn't notice for ages 'cos we were bickering, until suddenly we heard a crash and people screaming but by this point it was too late. Me and Carrie ran into the next room marked STAFF CATERING but OH MY DAYZ, by this point it weren't a pretty sight. Lizanne and Clarrisa and Aled and all other TV crew were looking at us with thunderous expressions, holding empty plates and the entire floor was covered in a massive puddle of chicken curry. And my Penny was standing right in the middle of it all beside an upturned silver catering tray, licking it all up.

Oh Lord alive, I thought.

'Penny!' I shouted. 'What have you done?!'

'Your dog has stolen the whole crew's lunch and eaten it!' shouted the catering woman.

'Has she?' I said, trying to sound shocked. 'This is

proper out of character, she must be over-excited or something. . . . Penny, bad dog. Come here this minute!'

Penny just looked up from the curry for a second with a face that seemed to say, 'Jog on, bruv'.

'You have no control over that dog whatsoever, have you!?' said Clarissa, looking really annoyed.

'Not really,' I admitted, 'but she's a quick learner. That's why we're here!'

At this point Penny did what she likes to do best. She rolled on to her back and started wriggling around in the curry making a noise like a snorty pig.

'Oh, Penny, no,' sighed Carrie as her *Radio Times* cover modelling shoot disappeared before her eyes.

'I don't think this dog is suitable for *Doggy Detention*!' said Lizanne. 'She's too stubborn and too old to change her ways and to be quite frank, she's too fat. It would set a bad example to the dog owners of Britain.'

Well I started to get a bit angry then.

'She ain't fat! She's BIG BONED,' I said. 'Anyway, WHATEVER! I don't want to live in your bloody cobweb school! You can stick it up yer bum, bruv. Come on Penny, stand up, we're going home.' And I've no idea why, but Penny seemed to listen to that bit. She stood up and followed me. But as I reached the door I realised Carrie wasn't with me. She was still there pleading with the producers.

'But can't I still be in the show?' she was squeaking, 'My Alexis has natural star quality.'

'Oh we have a pretty blonde girl with a little yappy dog already,' said Clarissa, huffily. 'It was the two of you together as a pair or nothing at all.' I cringed a bit when she said that. Our *Doggy Detention* dream was very much over.

Well Carrie was LIVID. She stormed out of the room. 'Shiraz!' she said. 'Your dog has ruined everything. That was the start of my journey to proper fame there and now it's OVER! I'm getting the train home! I ain't getting in a car with that stupid mutt! It's covered in curry! It'll make my Lithuanian extensions smell funny!' Then she flounced off being all dramatic.

I couldn't help laughing. I mean it was all sort of hilarious when you think about it. Then I called up Wes and Bezzie and said we'd need to drive home via a BP garage and give Penny a pressure wash 'cos she was stinking to high heaven. At least Wes thought it was funny.

'No bother, innit,' he said and then he came and got me and Penny and drove us all home.

SUNDAY 20TH NOVEMBER

I was just reading back that last bit of my diary and I was nearly widdling myself laughing. Oh my days! All that *Doggy Detention* thing seemed proper serious at the time. Carrie went absolutely bananas, she did. Honest to God, she didn't speak to me for days and days! And the thing was, I wasn't exactly ringing her up being all grovelling beg-friendy going, 'Oh Carrie Draper please be my friend! Pleeeeeeease!' 'Cos sometimes Carrie needs to realise that life ain't all about Princess Carrie getting her own way all the time. Bad stuff happens and what will be will be, etc. I try to be a bit harder on Carrie now 'cos she can proper take advantage. The thing with Carrie Draper is she finds it hard to think outside of Carrieworld and about other people's needs and wants. It's like she's in a little bubble sometimes and the world just revolves around her. She acts like a celebrity when she ain't even one!

Luckily I'm used to dealing with her primadonna moments.

And I'm bloody glad we never went on *Doggy Detention* anyway. The only good thing about the whole thing would have been moving into the school and out of Thundersley Road for a few weeks. 'Cos even a creaky boarding school with cobwebs and spiders would be better than living squashed up in this tiny house with two adults, four nearly-adults, one baby and a dog living here!

I can hardly stand it any more! THUNDERSLEY ROAD IS OFFICIALLY FULL. And today, Sunday, Nan, Clement and Wes came round for their Sunday dinners too. We have the Wood Sunday dinner in two rooms now, the living room and the kitchen, and someone has to go running room to room with the gravy jug! And everyone keeps swapping seats all the time like musical chairs so someone can feed Fin or be near Clement to speak to him 'cos he gets deafer by the day! And everyone's mobile phones are bleeping with texts and the omnibus of *EastEnders* is usually on with no one watching it and Fin is usually screaming and the Jehovahs Witness religious bods usually land on the front doorstep right at the moment when we've all got our grub. And if Murph is feeling mischievous he sometimes invites them in shouting, 'Come in! Yeah, there's ten people in here that all want to be converted! 'Ere you're going to hit the jackpot here, bruv!'

So much for Sunday being a chilled out 'day of rest'. It's like eating at Liverpool Street Station during rush hour!

I mean, today I took my eye off my dinner for five seconds and when I looked back one of my roast spuds had been thieved! The best one! The crispiest one! Obviously it was Murphy. So I pretended I hadn't seen and I kept my face proper straight and waited until he weren't concentrating then I stuck TWO EXTRA BRUSSEL SPROUTS back on his. HAHHAHAHAH! Well, Murph was proper fizzing then 'cos our nan saw him with the leftover sprouts and she gets all funny peculiar about people not eating all their vegetables. So he had to eat them! Amazing! The thing is any fool knows that a Brussel sprout ain't a real vegetable, is it? It's a joke vegetable which tastes of bogies and farts that we're made to eat by our parents 'cos they resent us for turning up in their lives and stopping them having any fun for ever, innit? This is my theory I have been working on for some time. Has anyone ever seen an adult actually eating a Brussel sprout themselves? 'Course they haven't. It's all a scam, bruv. I wrote to the Discovery Channel about this once and suggested they do some sort of documentary about it, but up to now there's been no reply. All these TV people are right clowns.

Anyway, this house is now officially too hectic to be dealing with. And there's no danger of it getting any less crowded either 'cos Ritu from Japan is well in my mother's good books right now as she's pretty much stamped out my brother's involvement with the Thundersley Road Man Dem. That was my brother's gang that he was in last year. Except they weren't really a gang. It was just his mates Tariq and Sizzle overdosing on too much Channel U and trying to start up some postcode war stopping kids from coming down Thundersley Road for fear of 'getting merked'. Well this seemed like a proper pointless threat to me anyway. What kid in their right mind would come down Thundersley Road by choice anyway? Especially now that Clinton Brunton-Fletcher is locked up and not selling any weed no more? And as far as I know, Rose, who is Clinton and Uma's mother, is only selling cocaine now and she's not selling it to kids 'cos she was telling Uma she feels she's got a 'social resonsibility not to'. Uma told me that on the phone the other night from Kensington. Uma didn't sound too impressed. She said she reckoned her mother would be more responsible if she stopped selling bloody drugs altogether, and better still took those net curtains down from the front bay windows and gave them a good boil wash 'cos they're filthy, 'the mucky bleeding cow'.

Uma is sick to death of her family. Uma says she gives up with them. I was really glad right then that I'd promised Kez I wouldn't tell anyone her secret. I don't think it would have cheered Uma up at all.

I promised Uma I'd go to stay with her in her new flat in London proper soon. It's hard, though 'cos Uma works nights in the casino and I work days with the babies. I miss Uma so much. I miss wandering down to her house and doing our English AS coursework together. And I miss her being so clever and 'resourceful', as Ms Bracket would say. Me and Uma used to have a right laugh.

Truth to tell, I'm proper bored here in Goodmayes.

The only thing that's happened down Thundersley Road in the last few days was the Brunton-Fletcher twins running about with no shoes on chucking stones at cars and Old Bert at Number 89 coming out in his underpants with a bag of Mighty White bread made into crumbs then scattering it everywhere for the pigeons. Then his next-door neighbour Tricia who works down Netto came running out shouting, 'They're just bloody rats with wings you stupid old fart!' And then the council officers came down again to investigate and everyone went out in their gardens to watch the shouting. Honest to God, that's the most exciting thing that has happened here since August, when I got back from Ibiza! And worst of all I'm trapped here right in the middle of it. WHY DID I NOT FINISH MY A-LEVELS?! I MUGGED MYSELF OFF LIKE A RIGHT PLANT POT THERE DIDN'T I?! I know I did.

WEDNESDAY 23RD NOVEMBER

11pm – Thundersley Road.

I've just been round Draperville this evening with Kez to see Carrie. We went round there on a mission to be frank, 'cos Kez rang me this morning after she'd just bumped into Carrie in Ilford X-change outside Holland and Barrett. Kez reckoned Carrie weren't looking too happy. Kez said Carrie's eyes were kind of hollow like she was sad to see her. So Kez says to Carrie, ''Ere what's up with your face mush, have I done something to offend you?'

And Carrie says, 'Don't be daft, Kez. I just didn't recognise you until you were up close. I'm proper tired 'cos I'm on a detox.'

So Kez says to Carrie, 'Oh I went on a detox once. I stopped drinking alcopops and Aftershock and just stuck to pure spirits like vodka and Bacardi instead.'

Well apparently Carrie said, 'No, Kez, not that type of detox. A proper detox where you just drink boiling water with honey and special vitamins in it that takes all the inpurities out of your skin and makes it glow and helps you drop a few pounds in weight too.'

'Oh my DAYZ,' I said to Kez when I heard that. ''Ere she didn't mention that this detox would stop her knee turning inwards and make her face less lopsided by any chance?'

'Eh?' says Kez, sounding a bit shocked I could be so nasty. 'What you talking about? There's nothing wrong with her knee or her face!'

'I KNOW THAT!' I said to Kez. 'I know! It's ever since she went to that bloody *Supermodel Unmasked* thing and the judges all laughed at her. Her head's gone a bit wonky. I dunno what to do with her! She reckons she's fine but I don't think she is.'

'Aw, Shiz, she'll get over it,' Kez said to me. 'I mean, remember when I was with my babyfather Luther in Year Eleven and he got me pregnant, eh? And then I got fatter and fatter and I was well paranoid, but Luther, he says don't be daft 'cos he proper loved me and I was beautiful and he'd never leave me, and then I had Tiq and he ran off! And he never spoke to me ever again and got his bloody mother to come round and dump me and say he'd gone in the navy! Well my head was all over the place after that weren't it, Shiz? I thought I was a right munter. I couldn't stop crying for weeks!'

'Yeah,' I said. 'That was proper heavy, Kez.'

'Point is, I got over it though, didn't I?' she said.

'How?' I said.

'I just got really hammered off my head a lot on booze,' she said. I sighed when she said that.

'And what happened after that, Kez?' I said, pushing her a bit for the answer I wanted to hear her say.

'And then I got up the duff again, innit!' she laughed. 'Oh my dayz, I'm a proper doughnut innit?'

'Some might say that, Kez,' I said giggling. 'I ain't giving a comment.' Kez giggled a bit, too, even though deep down it was the proper opposite of funny.

''Ere Miss Clever-Arse,' Kez said to me. 'So shall we go round and see Carrie this evening or what?'

'Yeah,' I said. 'But listen, I'll be in charge of giving out the advice right? You, Miss Yoyo-Knickers, can just keep quiet.'

Well Kezia nearly wet herself laughing at that.

'Deal,' she said.

We got to Carrie's at about 8pm tonight and walked up the gravel drive just as Maria was getting out of her jeep, looking all skinny and young with two of those big posh shopping bags, made of cardboard, tied with ribbons, that you get from expensive clothes shops. Maria looked at me and Kez and sort of waved. She was staring mostly though. Staring at Kez. She was giving Kez a funny look as if to say, 'What are you doing inside my gates? You do not fit with my cream world and white walls and special porcelaine stalactite ceiling that I have had done in my lounge area 'cos I saw it in *Hello!* magazine. You are a teenage mum who's expecting another kid, dressed in a red, gold and green crop top with the slogan, "Bestest Babymama in Town" written across the front!'

So I says, 'Alright, Maria.' I gave her a look back which meant something like, ''Ere Maria, don't be giving it the big one like Kez is common and you're not common too, 'cos my mother reckons that back in the 1980s, before you married Barney, you were absolutely broke! My mother reckons that she once lent you a fiver till pay day 'cos you didn't have no electricity and you'd been living in the dark and turning up for work behind the bar at the Goodmayes Social with your lipstick on all wonky! And being proper honest, Maria, if you've got anything to say about the way Kez lives well maybe you should be looking closer to home at your own daughter 'cos she's indoors now drinking syrup water making herself ill!'

But I just thought that. Obviously. I didn't say it.

And the minute it flashed across my mind I thought to myself, 'OH MY DAYZ Shiraz Bailey Wood! You're turning into your mother! That's exactly the type of thing she would say!!' I hear myself say stuff like that a lot and it is well freaky. Like the other day I was in ASDA with Cava-Sue and we were taking the stuff out of the trolley and putting it on the conveyorbelt and Cava-Sue was standing all the bottles up straight.

'Cava-Sue! Lay the bottles down flat!' I said. 'They'll just fall over and smash and then we'll have to pay for them!' Well Cava-Sue just looks at me and smirks. 'All right, Diane! Mother! Hello? is that you in there?'

So I went bright red! But then later on when we were unpacking the shopping, Cava-Sue picks up the crappy supermarket brand orange squash I'd put in and she goes, 'There's no point in buying this stuff, Shiraz, you just have to use the double the amount. It's a false economy!'

HA HA HA 'It's a false economy!' Just like my mother always says. Amazing! We're both turning into her! Thank God it's not just me.

I was thinking about this while watching Maria walking into Draperville looking all skinny and perfect. As Carrie is getting older I reckon she and Maria are beginning to look more like sisters than mum and daughter. To be honest, I hope Carrie don't ever turn into her mother properly, 'cos I don't think Maria is very happy deep down. She just seems to drive around all day in her jeep thinking of stuff to spend money on and then getting it and thinking of other things to spend more. I don't reckon that's happiness though, is it? Happiness is about being happy, innit. Laughing and smiling and that.

Me and Kez walked into Draperville and found Caz in the lounge area watching the massive flatscreen TV that Barney treated himself to last month. I don't know what happened to the last widescreen telly he had. It's probably in the garage gathering dust. I'm going to tell Cava-Sue, she's always good at finding homes for stuff the Drapers don't want.

Anyway, we found Carrie lying on the sofa with a little duvet pulled around her 'cos she reckoned it was cold. It wasn't cold at all. In fact me and Kez had just been saying how freakishly not-cold it was for November.

'Whatup Cazza?' I said, wandering in and plonking myself down on Barney's special LazyBoy chair. I grabbed the remote control and brought the feet rest up and put the back down, then turned the vibrating massager seat bit on, then I lay almost horizontal while the chair juddered, looking at Carrie waiting for an answer. Kez sat on the sofa beside Carrie proper staring at her. Carrie looks a bit weird at the moment. She's just two massive big blue eyes in a tiny face on top of a skinny body. She says she's a size six right now. Well if this is a size six I don't want to know what size zero looks like. Just a skeleton dipped in fake tan, I reckon.

'Aight,' says Carrie, a bit quietly.

'How are you feeling today?' I said.

'I'm fine,' Carrie says, 'Why wouldn't I be? What's going on?'

'Nothing,' Kez says. 'We just thought we'd come over and say hello. You looked a bit weird this morning, innit.'

'Oh that was that detox thing,' Carrie says. 'I've come off it now. I just had some toast and jam and a Kit Kat. I sort of fell over in the kitchen just before. Mrs Raziq went mental and made me eat something.'

'What do you mean, you "sort of fell over"?' I said to her.

'Oh, it was nothing,' Carrie said. 'It just went all, like, black, like shadows, around my eyes for a second and then I felt all hot and then I woke up and I was lying on the floor and Mrs Raziq was making a right old fuss.'

'You fainted 'cos you've not been eating.' I tutted.

'Nah, I don't think it was that Shizzle,' Carrie says. 'I think it was just all the poisonous toxins vacating my body. 'Cos honest to God I feel quite good now. I feel proper lively. I think it's worked!'

Kez sucked her teeth a bit and said, 'Carrie, you feel lively 'cos you just put some bread and jam and chocolate in your belly, innit. That's pure energy, ain't it? Bruv, I spent every GCSE science class smoking ciggies in the supplies cupboard and getting off with Luther and even I know that.'

Well Carrie just ignored that and turned the channel over to ITV2 where they were playing a rerun of *Tiffany Poole: Uncovered*. It's an hour-long documentary about Tiffany Poole and her whole empire and how amazing she is to manage to be so beautiful, as well as a bikini designer, and a best selling author, and a mother to three children, and a fitness and diet guru, AS WELL AS one of the richest women in Britain who does lots of amazing work for charity.

We all watched it for a while saying nothing. It was difficult not to get proper mesmerised by the programme 'cos Tiffany's life is like a dream really. Nothing bad ever seems to happen. Her house is in Surrey close to somewhere called Godalming. It is absolutely enormously massive with loads of space for all of her family to spread out. She's got a massive long dining table where everyone eats together and her showbiz mates are always popping round. Tiffany is an amazing cook too, by the way. She can whip up a dinner for twenty people who've just popped by unexpectedly in under half an hour and she doesn't even get stressed. And she has a solid silver gravy jug! She don't just use an old measuring jug with felt tip pen marks on it like we do at our house. Tiffany also has a stable with horses, and some rescued donkeys in a field eating organic carrots, and a heated swimming pool in the basement, where she swims fifty lengths every morning to keep her physique in size zero shape for modelling! I swear, none of us could take our eyes off the screen.

'I think I've just been a bit, well, depressed recently,' Caz said suddenly to us both. 'Y'know I think I reckoned this showbiz thing would be a lot easier to break into. I just keep getting rejected. I ain't good enough to do anything. I've been working flat out for weeks now and my profile ain't raised any higher at all!'

Well this was true, I couldn't argue with her. Carrie was not one smidgeon more famous now than when she got back from Ibiza. In fact she was LESS famous now 'cos no newspapers wanted her Ibizan prison story at all now. But I didn't know what to say to her. I couldn't give her any proper advice 'cos I don't even know what it was that

Carrie wants to be. She hasn't got a specific talent! She can't really sing or dance or act! She just wants to be famous and have people recognise her. I don't know how you do that!

At this point the TV show came to an end and the credits were rolling across the screen and then a big booming voiceover said, 'Would you like to live the Tiffany Poole lifestyle!? Are you eighteen to twenty-five!? Could you cope with everything the celebrity life throws at you and keep your feet on the ground!? Could you be Tiffany Poole's personal assistant?! Well this spring, ITV2 and Tiffany Poole are searching for the perfect person for the job! And we'll be filming all the adventures for our new show coming soon: *Tiffany Poole: Help Me I'm a Celebrity*! Go to www.tiffanypoole.com/helpme for details!'

Well Carrie sat bolt upright on the sofa when she heard that. She pressed record on the Sky Plus box, then she rewound it and played the bit again.

'Oh my God!' she said.

'NO,' I said.

'I could do that! I'm going to apply!' said Carrie. 'You could come with me and—'

'Carrie Draper,' I said. 'NO. I'm NOT, no, absolutely NOT. No way am I coming with you to any more reality TV auditions! And that's final. And I don't think you should go anyway. They're bad for your health. And that's the matter closed. It's a NO from me Carrie, sorry.'

'Oh, go on!' Carrie said, grabbing her MacBook Air and looking up the website.

'I mean it, Carrie. I won't be talked into this one,' I said. 'Kez? You agree with me don't you?'

'Yeah,' said Kez.

'We've had enough of all this now Carrie. It's time you forget about all this fame business and start keeping it real!'

And I meant it this time. I really, really, really meant it. End of.

DECEMBER

WEDNESDAY 7TH DECEMBER

I suppose one good thing that came out of today was that I got to see Godalming. It was quite pretty, especially today 'cos it was wintery, so there was frost on the fields and the trees like on a Christmas card. Godalming is a little town in a county called Surrey near London. Surrey is sort of on the other side of London to Essex. I've never been to Surrey before today. I never really fancied going until today, 'cos when I was little I asked my mother what Surrey was like and she said, 'Pgh! Surrey?! It's just like Essex but totally up itself. Better off not giving it the time of day I reckon!'

I've started realising of late that my mother can be very negative. Sometimes it's better to make your own mind up about stuff. Anyway, Surrey seemed OK. Not as good as Essex, though, 'cos Essex RULES. The best bit about Godalming I reckon was that it had a bare good chip shop with amazing battered sausages. Thick, crunchy batter, really meaty tasty sausages, and plenty of salt. I'd go back just for one of them.

Surrey is also where Tiffany Poole's place Mandalay Manor is. Tiffany Poole lives in a ginormous white mansion with about twelve bedrooms and turrets like a fairytale castle and long black tarmac drive. The whole place is surrounded by green fields. I ain't ever been fussed about fairytales myself, I've not got time for Prince Charmings and poison apples and all that guff, but even I thought this place was pretty amazing. Carrie LOVED it. A tear actually dripped down her cheek when she saw it. 'It's just like I always dreamed it would be!' Carrie said. 'I feel like this is the first step of my journey! My journey to fulfilling my dream!' Carrie speaks like this a lot now. Like she's on a reality TV show, even though she's not on one. She's always going on about 'learning about myself', and 'giving it 110%', and 'her great journey', and 'tackling her fears', and 'doing this to make her dad proud.'

And I'm all like, 'Carrie, bruv, I only asked you if you wanted a can of Fanta. Calm down, no one's bloody filming you!'

I wasn't even planning on going to Godalming today to that stupid, *Tiffany Poole: Help Me I'm a Celebrity!* audition. It just sort of happened. I only went because a) Carrie has moaned on about it every bloody day FOR WEEKS! And as it got closer the moaning got proper intense. Especially after she sent in an internet application and got sent all the details and directions. By that point she'd stepped her moaning up a gear from a high-pitched bleat to a low-pitched continual nag. VERY ANNOYING. And b) the cheeky mare started chucking in phrases like, 'If you cared about me, Shiz, you'd come with me!' and 'Of all the times to let me down now, Shizzle, who'd have guessed it would be NOW on this stage of MY JOURNEY? At this LIFE CHANGING moment in my life? Just as I'm off to work for Tiffany Poole!', and 'Well it takes times like this to work out who your REAL FRIENDS are! Don't it?'

Luckily I didn't slap her. I felt like it, but I didn't. Violence is never the solution, me and Uma have agreed this is one of our key rules in life. And YES I felt like shaking Carrie, really hard, till all her hair extensions rattled about like she was in a tornado. But I didn't. GO ME!!!

But the final straw came last night when I was round Draperville watching Carrie working out the route from Goodmayes to Godalming. OH MY DAYZ IT WAS PAINFUL. At one point she had out her MacBook Air plus her Blackberry Plus, and an A4 notebook covered in confused scribbles in front of her. Plus she was on the phone to National Rail enquiries squeaking, 'Just tell me which trains! Oh my gosh! How? Change where? Which part of Waterloo Station? How will I know which platform? What do you mean look at the big overhead information boards like everyone else has to? Which boards!? How will I know where to look?!'

By this point, I shouted, 'OK ENOUGH, STOP IT!' and I had to get involved. I couldn't help myself. It's all this looking after babies lark I do, innit? It makes me proper interfering. I can't stop taking charge of things.

It's like I find myself opening cartons of orange juice for people, and asking them if they need the toilet before we set off somewhere, and wiping food dribbles off their faces, like I'm their bloody mother! Carrie loves all that, though. She needs a personal assistant more than Tiffany Poole. If we could get Barney to pay me to look after Carrie then we'd both be laughing.

As I was eating my Aldi Chocobangbangs this morning, my family were widdling themselves laughing just at the thought of Carrie Draper being a 'personal assistant'. Our Murph was coming out with all sorts of stories about Carrie we'd all forgotten. Our Murph's got a memory like an elephant for embarrassing stuff. That's why you should never bother arguing with him 'cos you'll end up getting owned. Like I'd clean forgotten about that time last year when Carrie took the WRONG DOG home from Goodmayes Park. She DOGNAPPED some old dear's dog! And she didn't even realise until the woman rang up Maria and screamed, 'I'm calling the number I've found on a Chihuahua's collar! Do you own a dog called Alexis!? Because I've got her with me now! Someone has just taken my dog by accident! It was a tall blonde girl! She was chatting to one of the park gardeners in the park while our dogs were both playing together! And then she STOLE my dog!'

Well it turned out Carrie was out walking Alexis when she spotted Cotch, this boy she fancied, digging the flowerbed on the park. Cotch was doing some community service hours for selling weed and Caz reckoned he looked bare fit in his council regulation community service overalls. In fact she was so busy flirting with him that when she set off home she didn't realise she'd picked up the wrong dog! She walked the half mile back to Draperville with a proper confused Jack Russell dog yapping away in a pink basket. How did she not notice?!

'I had my iPod on,' Carrie said to me later. 'I just proper zoned out.'

'Oh my God!' Cava-Sue said this morning, her eyes watering from laughing. 'Has Tiffany Poole got any pets for Carrie to lose then?'

'She's got a poodle,' said my mother. 'I know that. It's called Trixie. I saw her with it on a chat show. It did a poo on Jonathan Ross's desk.'

'Yeah, and she's got some horses too,' said Murphy. 'I watched a show about her once on ITV2.'

'Murph?' I said, 'What were you doing watching a show about Tiffany Poole?'

'It was the one where she was, erm, shooting all the bikini pictures for her calendar,' said Murphy. 'It was quite, erm, interesting, y'know? I'm interested in, erm, photography!'

Well my dad started laughing then. 'Oh I think I saw that one too, son! My Lord, you don't get many of those to the pound, do you?!' My dad mimed the shape of a woman with large gazongas. Well Murph started laughing

131

and saying, ' 'Ere Dad, she was never going to drown with THOSE inflatable waterwings, was she?' And then the two of them laughed their blokey laughs and my mother told them to both shut up and stop being rude.

One thing's for sure though, everyone in my family seemed to know a bit about Tiffany Poole. In fact this was one of the best conversations our family had together for ages 'cos all of us seemed to have an opinion on how Tiffany lived her life.

'Those boobs aren't even real!' my mother was saying. 'If she keeps messing about with them she's gonna end up with that MRSA superbug thing! That killed your nan's friend Doris! She'll be sorry then!'

I sort of agreed with that. My mother and me once watched a show where Tiffany was having her new boob saline bags put in. It was called *Tiffany Poole: Under the Knife.* It was on E4. About three weeks after the operation Tiffany decided she didn't like the size of them and wanted bigger ones! So she went in and got cut open and sewed back together again. All the blood and stitches was well minging. I'd rather have my normal boring boobs than go through all that pain.

So then our Cava-Sue was chipping in. 'Well it's Tiffany Poole's body and her right to do whatever she wants, Mother! I mean in a way, if you look at all the businesses she runs at once, she's a 21st century feminist icon!'

Murph grunted and says to me, ' 'Ere Shiz, if you

meet her will you ask her if she's going to do any more topless horse-riding shots, 'cos they were WELL GOOD and I bought the magazine they were in, but then Tariq stole it.'

'Yeah Murph,' I said. 'That'll be my opening question, obviously.'

Me and Carrie set off to Godalming at about 9am this morning. Carrie was determined to be one of the first in the queue. I've honestly never seen her so focussed. This whole thing really mattered to her. Carrie seemed to think *Help Me I'm a Celebrity!* would be a great 'career move' as it would really 'showcase all her talents' and really get her 'networking in the right circles'.

To be frank, I thought it was another massive waste of time. I didn't say that though, 'cos Carrie's a bit fragile of late. And then when we got to Godalming and took the minibus shuttle service to Mandalay Manor, I gave up hope altogether. The bus was full of some well irritating girls being all loud, and singing and show-bizzy. And some of them had four years experience of personal assisting! Some had even worked with celebrities and knew all the ins and outs of the job. Like how to arrange for a helicopter to land on a mansion roof at midnight. Or where to find a macrobiotic protein shake at 3am in Los Angeles. Or how to fool paparazzi photographers by sneaking out of a restaurant back door into a waiting getaway car.

As they all nattered away to each other, Carrie got quieter and quieter. Then we arrived at Mandalay Manor and saw about FIVE HUNDRED girls all queuing down the driveway and Carrie stopped speaking altogether. I sat and stared out of the minibus window at the horses and donkeys in the field and hoped I could get Carrie in and out of this place as soon as possible, 'cos I was starving and I fancied a battered sausage from Mr Yolk's for my lunch.

Well what happened next was a bit of a blur. Me and Caz went to the back of the queue and soon loads more girls arrived in minibuses and coaches, until the queue behind us was twice as long again. Then suddenly, the manor doors flung opened and it all went a bit mental. The queue started moving forward really quickly. I stood beside Carrie right at the front, and this flustered-looking TV producer woman said to me, 'OK, here's your badge, write your name on it please and stick it on. And here's your wristband! Yes, you with the brown hair and the hoodie, go to Room 3 and fill out these forms! Blondie in the pink coat go to Room 7 and fill out these forms!'

'Oh I'm not auditioning!' I said, pointing at Carrie. 'I'm with her.'

'What? Well you can't go in then. You'll have to leave the manor house now and wait outside for her! That's the rules.'

'How long will she be?' I asked. 'It's December! It's cold out there!'

'Tsk,' tutted the woman. 'I have no idea. Any time between twenty minutes and four hours. We've no way of knowing. It depends how far you get in the process. Look are you doing it or not? You're holding up the queue!'

Well, Carrie had shot off into Room 7 by then. Before I knew it, I was sat in Room 3, filling some forms out. It was better than hanging about in the frost outside, I thought.

I suppose another good thing about today was that it made me think about what my 'skills' are. I didn't think I had any actual skills. I thought they were just something boffins had. But when I was trapped there in that room, staring at a big white sheet of paper with the question, 'What are your skills?' on it, it was amazing the stuff that popped up in my brain. For example, in London, when I worked at Sunshine Sandwiches on the help desk I definitely learned office skills. Stuff like how to take phone messages and send emails and how to unblock the IT department's annoying security firewall thingy so I could go on MSN and Bebo and chat to Carrie. And yes, OK, fair play, I got fired from Sunshine Sandwiches and told to never darken their doors again, but it was still 'work experience'! And when I worked on the London Eye as a guide, I totally 'refined my communication skills' by telling thousands of tourists about London landmarks and 'enhancing their sightseeing experience'. And OK, YES, again, I got the boot from there too for making up lies about the Houses of Parliament and St Paul's Cathedral which eventually led to a massive enquiry within the London Eye Head Office into how someone as under qualified as me was let loose with the public. HOWEVER, in my defence I was only doing my best to make people enjoy their holiday in Great Britain! It wasn't just 'Great Britain' that summer. I made it into 'Bloody-great-in-fact-proper-bare-jokes Britain!' And when I worked at Mr Yolk, I learned how to make a fried egg bap and a cup of tea in two minutes forty-seven seconds flat while bootiebouncing to Cicada on Kiss FM. And when I worked at the House of Hardy Christmas grotto I learned how to stay calm and patient even when a child has just chundered a Happy Meal down my special velvet all-day stay-puffed pantaloons. And when I was at *London Alive*, I learned how a newspaper is put together, and best of all, I learned how to communicate in 'an original and entertaining way' with the readers. I'm well proud of that. Anyway I wrote all this down on the form in my most rubbish handwriting, not even checking for spelling mistakes. Then I read it back and laughed, thinking I can't believe how much I rule. Oh and then I wrote down my GCSE grades and my AS-Level marks too 'cos I'm well proud of them and it felt good to write them on something 'cos no one seems to remember I passed them any more. Then I scribbled a whole load of other random words under the LIKES and DISLIKES section. Then finally under the space that said 'Why do you want to be Tiffany Poole's Personal Assistant?' I wrote in big block capitals:

I DON'T. I AIN'T FUSSED. I JUST WANT TO GET OUT OF THE COLD. I AIN'T FREEZING MY FANGITA. JOG ON, BRUV!

Then for the last five minutes I doodled and then I drew a brilliant picture of a squirrel eating a lollipop and coloured it in and then a woman with a clipboard turned up and took the sheets off me. Her perfume was so strong my eyes nearly started bleeding. ''Ere what's that you're wearing?' I asked, trying to sound like I liked it.

'It's called Gush by Tiffany Poole,' she said a bit snobbily. 'It's available to buy on your way out. It's forty seven pounds forty eight for 50ml of the eau de toilette.'

'Ooh, I'll be stocking up on that then,' I said. 'It's Christmas soon. I'll get one each for everyone in my family.'

She could tell I was taking the mick, 'cos she tutted at me and took my papers and clip-clopped off.

Honestly, I thought I'd get chucked out then, but I wasn't. I was told to go up the marble staircase to the ballroom for the next stage. This part was a 'group exercise' where me and eight other girls had to talk about ourselves. OH MY DAYZ, that was dull. All of these girls had been on a 'great journey' to get to this day and were 'going to give it 110%' and BLAH BLAH BLAH, and after about ten minutes I couldn't help myself and I said out loud, 'Look bruv, I don't want to wee on your bonfires, but you can't do anything 110%! That per cent don't exist. I got a C at GCSE Maths so I know that! Percentages only go up to 100% you total plant pots! Oh and by the way, you ain't all been on a great journey. You only came ten minutes up the road in an air-conditioned mini-bus! It ain't like you walked barefoot across India making people think twice about civil rights like Mahatma Ghandi did, innit!' Well none of the girls spoke to me after I said the Mahatmha Ghandi bit. I don't think they must have seen the documentary about him what I did. They all just turned their backs on me and wouldn't speak to me no more. It was a bit of a relief actually.

After that I got sent to another room and they filmed me talking about who I think I am. Then I was sent for a long chat with their resident psychologist, who didn't say hardly anything for a whole half hour and, believe me, by the time I left he looked more confused than I did. Then I got sent to do a general knowledge quiz, and by that point I was thinking. 'Where the heck is Carrie Draper?!' I'd not seen her for hours. We must have kept missing each other. This was starting to get silly.

Then the last part was all a bit trippy. I still don't believe it happened really. Basically two women in headsets came and escorted me into a downstairs living room. Inside sitting on a white sofa was Tiffany Poole!

Yes, real, live, in the flesh Tiffany Poole! Sitting right in front of me, with her hair up in a fancy beehive with curls in the fringe, wearing these amazing mega-bling diamond earrings and a shimmery long green skirt that looked a bit like a mermaid's tail. I felt a bit faint when I saw her, then I got myself together and did my best Uma Brunton-Fletcher 'you're not better than me' face.

Tiffany had on this pair of terrifying pointy six-inch black Louboutin high heels with red soles and diamonds all over the toes. She had loads of thick lip-gloss on that made her lips so big and shiny that I could nearly see my face in them! Oh and she's got even more massive boobs at the moment. She must have had new saline bags put in again. They were sticking out of the top of her black corset top.

Anyway, I didn't meet Tiffany Poole for very long – seven minutes maximum – and I don't think I made much of an impression. I couldn't work out what Tiffany Poole was really like deep down 'cos there was a load of other people with her speaking the words she needed to say for her like she had learning difficulties or something. Her manager and her PR woman kept saying stuff like, 'Hold it, can we cut filming here! Tiffany is getting a cold draft from somewhere! Is there a window open?' Or, 'Tiffany has a problem with how many bubbles are in the mineral water! She can only drink gently carbonated water! We have a problem here!'

Well it took me all my energy not to go, ''Ere mate,

you only have a problem with water if you have to walk six miles with your kids in the Darfur region of Africa to get it out of a muddy puddle wondering if you'll get blown up by a landmine on the way! I'm sure that water is fine to drink, bruv!'

But of course I didn't say that. Our Cava-Sue would have said it though. Cava-Sue says anything she likes. Just ask the kids from St Luke's infant school in Dagenham. Our Cava-Sue went through their lunchboxes last week and informed them that all their mummies were, 'in a sense, trying to murder you' by giving them unwashed fruit covered in chemicals! OH MY DAYZ that all kicked off big time! One mother chased Cava-Sue down the road as far as the lollypop crossing calling her 'an environmental Nazi' and smacked her with an umbrella! I didn't say anything as bad as that to Tiffany Poole. I was on my best behaviour.

Tiffany didn't say much to me really at all. When I walked in she just smiled a big wide smile with all her teeth showing, then someone said, 'This is Shiraz Bailey Wood.' And Tiffany smiled again and said, 'Charming name. Charming. Charming!'

'Shiraz is the girl who doesn't want to do the job, she's only here because she's cold,' said another woman in a beret.

Everyone laughed at this like it was solid gold jokes.

'What a brilliant sense of humour. Brilliant!' said Tiffany.

'How refreshing after all the people we've had today begging and crying,' said another woman.

'No, but that was the truth actually,' I said. 'I'm just here with my friend. I don't really know what I'm doing in here. I've been walking around this house doing tests for hours! I'm starving. Can I go soon 'cos I'm gonna get the shuttle bus back to town. I've got my eye on a battered sausage. And maybe a pickled egg too.' Well everyone laughed at that for ages like I was top of the bill at the Royal Variety Performance. I think I was a bit nervous actually. It was proper weird seeing someone as famous as Tiffany Poole right there in front of me. Like I'd jumped inside the television or something.

When eventually I was allowed to go I made my way out of the house and realised that almost all the other girls had vanished. The drive was really quiet, aside from TV people packing up vans. Then I spotted Carrie sitting on the side of the ornamental fountain looking proper miserable.

'Oi! Carrie! Hello!' I said. 'What did you think of Tiffany then!?'

'What?!' she said to me. 'I didn't see Tiffany. Is she even here?'

'Oh. How didn't you see her?!' I said.

'Shiraz,' Carrie said. 'I got kicked out after ten minutes. I only did the first round and then they said I wasn't needed any more. I've been waiting for ages.'

'Eh?' I said. 'How long have I been in there?!'

'Four and half hours,' she said. 'You're one of the last to come out.'

She didn't look very happy with me. In fact she looked quite cross. So I didn't mention anything about meeting Tiffany Poole. I didn't tell her anything at all.

THURSDAY 15TH DECEMBER

Tonight me and Cava-Sue went to the Mayflower Academy Winter Festival. Two little girls knocked on our door the other evening selling tickets. Four quid each they were! Me and Carrie and the gang used to do the festival for nothing when we were at Mayflower! I couldn't believe how tiny the girls were selling the tickets either.

'What year are you then? Year Seven?!' I said to them.

The girls just sucked their teeth at me and said 'We're Year Ten, blad, innit?' which made me feel proper freaked out, 'cos I'm sure I didn't look that small when I was in Year Ten. I felt a right old donkey. Then one of them pointed at Fin who I had under my arm and she said, 'When d'you have him then?'

'He ain't my baby!' I said huffily. They looked proper confused but I couldn't be arsed to explain.

'So what you doing this year then?' I said instead. 'I've organised the Winter Festival twice actually. Are you doing all the usual paperchains on the ceiling and carols and stuff?'

The girls looked at me like I was a proper dinosaur and said no, this year was going to be a multi-media presentation involving overhead screens, lighting displays and a live Skype link up with Afghanistan where Iqbal in Year Eleven's uncle lived, and Iqbal was going to recite a traditional hymn praising the glory of the prophet Mohammed, peace be upon him. The words were going to be emailed to everyone's phones and Blackberries beforehand so they could understand the message. Well I just sucked my teeth back at the girls then, 'cos to be honest their Winter Festival sounded well better than anything we did.

'So do you want some tickets or what?' one of them said, staring at Fin.

I was just about to say, 'No, bruv, I'd rather cut my own head off' when our Cava-Sue jumped in and bought two.

Cava-Sue was well excited about it. She was wigging on about how amazing it was 'supporting community well-being at a local level! Not just looking to central government to make social decay better!' Yes, she did actually say this. Basically Cava-Sue was saying that me and her going to the Winter Festival and paying four quid each to stand in a drafty sports hall, drinking mulled Ribena, watching Year Seven kids dressed as sheep, was somehow going to help the whole of Goodmayes in general. Like it was going to stop folk vandalising the bandstand in the park, and stop the kids on the Larkrise Estate merking each other over drug debt.

'How is it going to make it better?' I asked.

Cava-Sue sighed and said, 'It just is right!' and before I knew it we were on our way to Mayflower in the rain, pushing Fin in his buggy wearing a Santa hat, off to enjoy an evening of non-stop Winter Festival fun.

Fair play, I have to admit it. The festival *was* actually good fun. I liked the Skype link-up to Afghanistan and the dancing and the songs. And Ms Bracket the Headmistress did a good speech about how the past few years have been so important for Mayflower as it had finally started to shake off its 'Superchav' image because some amazing kids have worked so hard to turn perceptions around. They'd even had Prince Charles come to visit! Well I kept my head down when she was saying this as I didn't want her to notice me and remind her that I was one of the people who messed up and let her down.

Afterwards, it was nice seeing all sorts of people I'd not bumped into for ages, like Sonia Cathcart who used to be in my class and her mum and dad. Sonia looked totally different, too. More like a student. She had a rip in the knee of her jeans that I knew her mother was dying to sew a big JESUS IS ALIVE! patch over. The Cathcarts are well religious. They're Seventh Day Adventists. You see Mr and Mrs Cathcart down Ilford Mall sometimes holding signs that say, 'EVERYTHING IS ALL RIGHT!' So you walk past and think, 'How do they know?!' and then you realise that the message on their T-shirts says

'JESUS IS COMING!' As if, if I watch really closely, I'll see him walk past Claire's Accessories. I've not made up my mind about God yet, though sometimes I think it would be nice to really believe in something like that.

It turns out that Sonia passed her A-Levels and started studying a Theology BA Hons degree at a place called Leeds which is up north. I've never been up north but I have seen it on *Coronation Street* and it looks a bit weird 'cos all they do all day is stand in the pub or go over the road from the pub and order minicabs. And some of them keep pigeons in sheds as pets.

Anyway, Sonia said her mum and dad have helped her out financially with going to university 'cos they had some savings. She said she couldn't have done it without them, as she's had to pay rent and shell out for her books and her food and fees to the college and all the train fares to get there and back.

That blows my chances of going then. My mother is skint. She's been borrowing off ME lately! In fact, I need to start saving my wages properly. The whole family are tapping a fiver here and there right now, and most of the time they don't give it back! But they're family. They'd do the same for me, and it's for important stuff like food, and nappies and bills too. It's proper expensive just being alive sometimes. That's the only reason I'd want to be Tiffany Poole. Just to know what it's like to be able to pay for things and not worry.

Anyway, Sonia's theology degree sounded proper

interesting. It's all about studying what people from around the world think about God. I used to like Religious GCSE at school. Mrs Radowitz my old Religious Studies teacher was always saying I had a natural talent for it. Religion tells you a lot about different cultures, see. Why people do different things, like wear burkhas, or eat certain foods on certain days. It makes you more chilled out about it all instead of being scared of it.

Sonia asked me why I had never gone back and finished my A-Levels 'cos I was doing really well at them. 'You should be at university, Shiraz!' she said.

I don't know about that, but she had a point about the A-Levels, I suppose. I told her it just sort of never happened. Sonia said she reckoned the university part should happen one day and she was going to pray for me. 'Thanks, Sonia,' I said to her and when she walked off I felt a bit sad 'cos I thought it's going to take something bigger than praying to get me out of Goodmayes.

On the way out, Ms Bracket grabbed me by the arm and said, 'Shiraz Bailey Wood, I don't believe it! Hello! How are you doing, young lady!?'

For some season I felt well embarrassed. 'Oh, I'm OK!' I said, 'I'm fine!'

She smiled one of her lovely warm smiles and said, 'I was looking out for you re-joining us this September! But then I thought, well, I know Shiraz, she's obviously doing her own thing. You were always a free spirit. Where are you working now? Are you still in London?'

'Erm, yeah,' I said. I can't believe I lied to Ms Bracket. 'Yeah, I work as an, erm, personal assistant. I'm loving it!'

'Oh? Really?!' she said to me. 'That's good news. I'm so glad you're happy! And the thing is, when the mood takes you, you could always go back to college, top up those grades, then who knows, take a degree? You were always a bright spark, Shiraz Bailey Wood! Remember, you're the master of your own destiny!'

'Yeah, I know Ms Bracket, lovely to see you,' I said, and I got away as fast as I could.

After me and Cava-Sue left the Winter Festival, I was well quiet 'cos my head was spinning. Cava-Sue wanted to get the bus down into Ilford for a bit 'cos it was late-night shopping, so I went with her. It was quite miserable really 'cos the streets were proper mobbed with people and it was raining quite hard and we didn't have an umbrella, not that Fin cared 'cos he had the front plastic bit down on his buggy and he was in there in a Santa hat and a scarf, as warm as toast.

It was when we were coming out of Boots, weighed down with three-for-the-price-of-two bubble baths and footscrubs and tubes of wrapping paper, that Cava-Sue let out a squeak and said, 'Oh my God, Shiraz, look! Look! It's Wesley Barrington Bains II. Over there! He's in H Samuels the jewellers. What's he buying?'

So we crept a bit closer and that's when I saw something that made me go proper freezing cold. He was looking at the section of platinum engagement rings.

'Come on, Cava-Sue!' I said, pulling her arm and making her walk with me fast in the opposite direction. 'Just bloody come on.'

CHRISTMAS EVE

11.15pm

The freakiest thing ever just happened.

And I mean EVER EVER EVER! My hands are shaking and I feel proper vomity. I can't believe Carrie just ran her mouth off at me like that down the phone. OH MY DAYZ Carrie!?? Can't you see this is hard for me too?! I didn't expect any of this to happen! You can't go shouting nasty names like that and not expect me to bloody shout back at you either!

And yeah, I know I ran my mouth off back at you like a rudegirl and said all sorts of stuff that was horrible, but honest to God you pushed me to it! You called me a selfish bitch! How can I be a selfish bitch? You're the one acting like a bitch. Your head ain't working straight any more. You need to quit that stupid size zero diet! 'Cos size zero ain't just your dress size now, it's the number of braincells you got left too! And I'm sorry if that's cruel but it's the solid gold truth. I'm only keeping it real. Oh God, my stomach is bubbling, I think I'm going to puke.

Basically, it was just a normal Christmas Eve in the Wood house. I was standing in the kitchen wrapping a big box of Cadbury's Fingers in sparkly wrapping paper for my mother, which was a pressie from our Penny. Me and Cava-Sue were singing to Mariah Carey, 'All I Want for Christmas' on Essex FM and trying to stop greedyguts Murphy from opening the tin of Quality Street early to thieve all the green triangles and toffee barrels. Murphy was reminding Ritu about how depressing *EastEnders* on Christmas Day was going to be, again, with at least one death and maybe two murders. The dog was walking about hoovering up stray food where she could find it, when suddenly there's a buzz at the door.

Well my mother starts shouting, 'Shiraz! There's someone at the door!!'

'Well, can you not answer it yourself, Mother? It'll be Aunty Glo won't it?' I shouted.

'Oh, it won't be for me, it'll be for one of you lot!' Mum said, sneaking a toffee barrel into her gob.

My mother has special X-ray vision when it suits her right enough.

So then we all bickered like that for a minute and then the doorbell buzzed again and eventually all the women joined forces and rounded on Murphy and agreed it would be for him.

So Murphy stands up and makes a big display of saying how downtrodden he is by all us females and he feels sorry for us all really being so LAZY and thunders into the corridor and opens the door and then suddenly he lets out a yelp. Then it all goes totally silent. Then there's another yelp!

'It must be Santa Claus with that Thomas the Tank Train Wash he wanted,' said my mother proper dryly and everyone started laughing.

But then Murphy sort of fell backwards into the living room and he said, 'Shiraz! It's erm, Tiffany, erm, I mean, Miss Poole, erm, sorry Mrs Tiffany . . . Shiraz, It's Tiffany Poole! IT'S BLOODY TIFFANY POOLE! AT THE DOOR NOW!!'

Well we all started to giggle 'cos this was obviously one of Murphy's jokes. But then a cameraman ran into the living room, followed by a woman in a headset with a clipboard who said, 'Hello, I'm Karen! Just pretend we're not here! Just act naturally!' She was followed by a soundman wearing headphones and waving a big long stick with a fuzzy thing. And then the most bizarre thing ever happened. Into our living room walked TIFFANY POOLE.

Well we all let out a bit of a scream. I sort of fell sideways in the kitchen doorway 'cos I was so shocked that I came over all faint. And my mother, who was still in her betting shop uniform midway through eating a plate of potato waffles with beans, stood up and put her hand out and sort of tried to curtsey! Cava-Sue and Ritu both kept trying speak but couldn't find any words. Our Penny was the only one who stayed cool! She just walked up and sniffed Tiffany's feet a bit then tried to nibble the corner of her handbag.

Tiffany Poole looked absolutely amazing. She had on a tight, black trouser suit and a little vest on covered in diamonds, and emerald-green stilettoes. Her hair was now a deep red colour. And it was shorter this time too, like she'd had all the hair extensions taken out and a blunt fringe cut at the front. She looked totally different to the last time I saw her. That's one of the reasons people love Tiffany Poole though, innit, 'cos she's always changing. She never stays the same. Whatever is the most fashionable way to look, that's what she looks like.

'Errrrrr, what are you doing here!?' I eventually got my head together enough to say. Tiffany just smiled her big wide smile and looked across to Karen with the clipboard and said, 'OK, shall I do that part now?' Karen gave her the thumbs up and Tiffany sort of bowed her head slightly and then looked up at me with her big eyes with her long eyelashes flapping and said, 'Shiraz Bailey Wood, it's been a very long journey for all of us. I know you've learned a lot about yourself. I know you stayed on your journey, no matter what, to make your family proud. I know you've given it 110%. And I'm thrilled to tell you that I think you've got the qualities I need to be the perfect personal assistant! So I've come to your home on Christmas Eve to ask you one important question. Shiraz Bailey Wood, will you come and live at Mandalay Manor and . . . help me, because I'm a celebrity!'

Well I just stood there for a bit with my gob open

staring at her. What the hell was she going on about? I haven't been on a great long journey! I told them at the audition I didn't want the job. If they'd not been laughing so much and saying I was a natural comedian who'd make great television, maybe they might have heard me! This was Carrie's dream job, not mine.

'Yes! Yes she will! She'll do it!' shouted Murph.

'She can start just after Christmas!' added my mother.

'Shiraz? What's going on?' Cava-Sue said, 'I didn't know you went for the job?!'

'Well, I sort of didn't . . .' I began to say, but then Karen butted in.

'Excuse me Shiraz, Tiffany has limited time as she needs to catch a flight, so is it OK if we film two endings and you can decide what you want to do later? Can we film one ending where you say "yes" and all your family cheer and then another ending where you say "no" and everyone looks unhappy, but still respects your decision and gives you a hug because this is the end of your great journey and you've still learned something about yourself? OK?!'

Well, that seemed the easiest way to do it 'cos my head was spinning and I didn't know what I wanted.

I just hadn't seen this coming! Even if Karen did remind me later on that when I'd been at Mandalay Manor I'd signed a form giving permission for a film crew to turn up at my house without any warning at any time they wanted. Plus I'd signed away all the rights not to be filmed or refuse the footage to be shown on the TV. I didn't remember signing that at all!

'It was on the back of sheet ten of the questions you filled in when you first got to the audition,' said Karen. I didn't check any of the backs of the sheets. I was too busy drawing the squirrel.

So we filmed two different endings.

For the 'yes' ending Tiffany kissed me on the cheek and said she was 'thrilled, simply thrilled', her lips were really cold and her cheekbone was really pointy as it clashed with mine. Then for the 'no' ending, suddenly, out of the blue, Tiffany started to cry. A little teardrop fell down her face and the cameraman took his lens really close and caught it! Then Tiffany said goodbye to us all and Karen escorted her to her limousine, that was outside waiting to take her to Heathrow with a big scary security man standing beside it swatting the Brunton-Fletcher kids off it like they were flies attacking a picnic.

I hoped Tiffany would make it for her flight in time as I didn't want to miss her spending Christmas with her family just 'cos of me.

I sat down on the sofa and my head was swimming. That's when Karen the producer had more time to explain what was happening. She said that I'd really shone at the auditions as I had a can-do attitude and a good sense of humour and 'great energy'. She said that if I said yes, I'd move into Mandalay Manor in my own loft apartment on January 3rd. She said I'd get my own

MacBook Air laptop, a daily allowance plus use of a driver to take me wherever I needed to go. In return I had to be filmed most days basically doing all of the jobs that Tiffany threw at me.

I asked Karen how long they needed me for and she said, well the series was due to 'TX in February and the season is eight episodes long, so we'll probably be wrapped by March.'

So I said, 'Sorry can you say that again so I understand it.'

Karen laughed and said, 'OK, it's quite simple, basically the show *Tiffany Poole: Help Me I'm a Celebrity* will start showing on TV in February. So that means we're filming now and will carry on filming until March.'

'Right, hang on a minute,' said Cava-Sue. 'So is this a real job or not? Or is it just for a TV show?' Well Karen sort of smiled and said, 'Of course it's a real job, but it's only a short contract. It depends on how Shiraz takes to her role as Tiffany's personal assistant whether she stays on full time forever or not. I mean, Tiffany has staff at Mandalay Manor that have worked with her for over a decade. It would be up to Tiffany to extend your contract.'

Then Murphy jumped in and said, 'Oh bloody hell you lot, why are you all going on about contracts! Shiraz, you nutjob! It's Tiffany Poole! Go and live in her house and help her do stuff she don't want to do! Bloody do it!!'

I looked at Murph and then I looked around at

everyone else all staring back at me. I didn't know what to say. So I ran upstairs and I picked up the phone and called Carrie. And I reckoned she might laugh and think it was proper funny. But she didn't. She went totally schizoid insane mental and said LOADS of nasty things to me.

Oh thinking about it makes me so bloody mad! How dare you, Carrie Draper?!! How dare you say I ain't a good, loyal friend to you! HOW DARE YOU?! You want to read through my old diaries, then you might see that crap I've put up with from you, you spoilt little madam! Well I've had enough of it all now. I'm not putting up with you any longer. This is a good opportunity for me. I need to get out of Goodmayes and let my brain expand a bit. You can't stop me doing that. I'm moving to Mandalay Manor and I won't be calling you, grovelling to be friends again, either! Actually, seeing as you've just told me not to speak to you again, FOR EVER, well I suppose you'll just have to watch me on telly to find out what happens next.

JANUARY

TUESDAY 3RD JANUARY

This is the first day of the rest of my life. I'm going on an important journey.

I would never say stuff like that usually 'cos it's well cheesy, but that's what Karen asked me to say today when I was standing outside our house on Thundersley Road before I got into the limousine to take me to Mandalay Manor.

Loads of folk in Thundersley Road came out to wave goodbye. The cameraman was over the moon. He said I could have an extra five minutes saying bye-bye to my family while he went and filmed all the 'colourful characters'.

Well he wasn't gone long 'cos Rose Brunton-Fletcher came out in her leather boob tube and leggings and asked him if he wanted to come in for 'a cup of coffee and a massage'. As far as I know, Rose Brunton-Fletcher is not a trained masseuse. Funny 'cos she certainly has a lot of men dropping by at the moment who seem to think she is. She must be learning to be one. Oh well, I suppose it's better than selling cocaine.

I felt a bit relieved when the limo came for me today 'cos I've been cooped up with my entire family in that house all Christmas. And I love my family, honest to God I do, I love the bones of them, but we'd all started doing each other's heads in. In fact we were sick of each other by Boxing Day and then we had to spend eight days together after that!

OH MY DAYZ! Our Murph is a proper nuisance, he's always hogging the telly for his Playstation and he plays it really loud so my head starts to hurt!

And Cava-Sue is always moaning at Lewis that she's tired and she could do with more help from him with the baby. And Fin can be a right brat sometimes, and the thing is I reckon it's Lewis's fault 'cos he never bloody says no to him, it's always yes, and it's making Fin a bit spoilt and tantrumy.

Well I don't say nothing to Cava-Sue and Lewis about it, but my mother gets proper stuck in giving advice, telling them about what it was like having a baby in her day, which makes them both go in the huff.

And Ritu is always misunderstanding stuff 'cos her English ain't great, so that means when I have a go at Murphy about him being selfish with the telly, Ritu needs it all explained to her, and then she takes Murphy's side in the argument so I go in the huff! And every time we all get over our huffs and agree on a TV show to watch together, my bloody father falls asleep in his chair and snores proper loud with his head back and his mouth open so we can't hear the programme, then my mother goes in the huff with him, and if my nan is round she goes in a huff with my mother for being nasty to Dad who is her son. What is my family like!? I'm sure other families aren't like this. I was reading *OK* magazine the other day and it was the Christmas special and it was full of famous people's family Christmases and they all just got along and sat around tables pulling crackers and smiling. They were all huff-free zones.

I suppose one good thing about the general fuss of a Wood family Christmas is I haven't had much time for many big heavy conversations with my Wesley.

I never told Wes I saw him in H Samuels that Christmas shopping night. And he never gave me a ring on Christmas Day. In fact, he got me a pair of really expensive GHD straighteners. That was a relief I suppose. I must have got it wrong, I reckon. Maybe I just freaked out and thought I saw what I didn't. Maybe he was just looking at something nice for his mother. He loves his mother Wesley does.

I told Wesley on Christmas Eve that I'd said yes to Tiffany Poole's offer and he went all quiet for a bit, but then he came to terms with it. Wesley says he ain't going to stop me doing the Tiffany Poole thing, but he needs to know that we've still got a future. He says he wants to know that we'll still stay together. 'That's the only thing I want to hear you say, innit,' he said.

So I said to him, 'Yeah, course we will, Wes, course we'll stay together.' But the truth is I don't really know what's going to happen. 'Cos this is the first day of the rest of my life, ain't it? I'm going on a journey. I'm sorry, Wes, but I need to concentrate 110%.

Midnight – Mandalay Manor.

I arrived at Mandalay Manor at about seven o clock tonight. OH MY DAYZ the mansion looked proper pretty as we drove towards it, all lit up with torches and spotlights lighting up the turrets. As we were driving there, the film crew filmed me talking about how excited I was to be meeting Tiffany again, then they filmed me getting out of the car and getting my suitcase and walking up the steps. And then when I got to the top of the steps Karen asked me if I wouldn't mind fastening my coat up to the top, then walking back down the steps pretending to be in a huff, and slamming the suitcase back in the boot so they could film me making an exit.

So I said, 'Why?'

'Well if you ever quit and run off in the middle of the night, we'll have this bit of footage on file so the viewer can get an idea how you did it. It just makes editing the whole storyline together easier. Can you fasten your jacket up so no one can really see what you're wearing so then it won't clash with whatever you might wear on your final day. Not that you're leaving soon, but it's just in case. Do you understand?'

I sort of did but I was getting quite confused by it all now. The whole day wasn't like reality at all. There were loads of stops and starts and filming things in two different ways 'just in case' and being asked to say stuff.

My head felt quite dizzy with it all. So anyway, I did what Karen asked and I acted my best 'I'm in a huff, I'm leaving' impression, and flounced down the stairs of Mandalay Manor and threw my suitcase in the boot, and the film crew laughed, and Karen said 'perfect'.

I felt a bit rubbish inside though 'cos this ain't Shiraz Bailey Wood. I'm all about keeping it real normally.

We went into the house through the big white double doors and a small woman called Maureen who was about sixty appeared and said hello and shook my hand. Maureen said she was Tiffany's housekeeper.

I smiled and said hello and stood there waiting for Tiffany to appear but she never did. Instead Karen popped up and said, 'OK, bye, Shiraz! See you tomorrow! Bright and early!? Thanks for everything!'

'Hang about,' I said. 'Am I not meeting Tiffany?'

'Oh no,' said Karen. Tiffany's not here she's erm, on a retreat. She's flying in tonight. We'll film the bits tomorrow where she meets you here in the hallway and shows you your new apartment and you run around screaming being excited! OK, have a nice night!'

Then the film crew packed up their Land Rover, and the limo disappeared into the garage, and then it was just me and Maureen stood there on our own. I felt proper homesick. My face must have shown it, 'cos Maureen said, 'Come on,' and led me into a big room with a massive long dining table in it. She pulled out two chairs then rang someone to bring us up a pot of tea and some scones and biscuits.

Then a butler arrived with them on a tray! I couldn't believe I was in the same dining room I'd seen on that episode of *Tiffany Poole: Uncovered*! The one with the long table I watched with Kez and Carrie. The weird things was, the table was quite dusty like it hadn't been used for ages.

'Those cleaners have obviously been slacking over Christmas!' said Maureen. She had one of those *Coronation Street* accents like my friend Danny has.

So I said, 'Maureen, did Tiffany not spend Christmas here then? Are all her family with her on the retreat?'

Well Maureen just sort of coughed a bit and said, 'No her family spent Christmas in Britain, Tiffany has been in South Africa.'

'That's a bit weird isn't it? This table is the perfect place for Christmas dinner. It's so long! And Tiffany loves to cook doesn't she?'

Well Maureen smiled and said, 'Gosh, I don't know when it was last used, this table.'

'Oh, I've seen it on a show being used! Tiffany cooked slow-roast leg of lamb with roast potatoes and mint sauce. Her whole family were here and her famous friends.' I said.

Maureen thought a bit and said, 'Ooh, hang on Shiraz, you're right! I know what you're referring to, dear! That was when she was promoting the Tiffany Poole Homeware Range wasn't it? The diamond encrusted pots and pans! Oh and those lovely silver gravy boats?'

'Yeah, that's it!' I said, 'Those amazing gravy boats. I wanted to get my mum one for Christmas but it was nearly fifty quid! So I got her some foot cream instead 'cos her heels are well hard like hooves.' Maureen laughed a lot at that.

On the walls in the dining room there was lots of family photos of Tiffany with her three children all hugging each other. Or Tiffany and her husband looking all loved up. So I asked if I'd meet any of them tonight and Maureen said that Olivia, who is fourteen, was in London at the moment because she was attending the *Vogue* Teen Fashion Party with Kitten Montague-Jones. And Tiffany's younger kiddies, Ophelia who is six and Digby who is four were asleep in their rooms on Floor Three which is the children's floor, with one of the team of nannies.

'Oh, right,' I said. 'And her husband's not here?'

'No, dear. He's in London staying at his friend's house.' Maureen looked a bit tired of all the questions. 'Right then, I expect, you want to see your apartment now?!' she said.

'Ooh, OK then!' I said. As we walked up the staircase I couldn't help thinking about that long dining table and thinking about how much fun the Wood family would have around it. We could skim the salt and pepper pots from one end to the other and my dad could stand up at the end and give one of his silly speeches that always ends with his 'Elvis on the toilet' impression. And if someone was doing your head in or had gone in a huff, well you could just move seats to another one about twenty-five metres away until they'd forgotten about their huff altogether!

We walked upstairs to the top floor and went into my loft apartment. It is absolutely totally amazing! I can't believe I'm sitting in it right now. It's got a big ginormous living room with a massive, squashy couch and a widescreen TV with one hundred channels and a DVD player with speakers in every room, and WiFi broadband, and a powershower, and steam room, and a four-poster bed, and a dressing table with bright lights around the mirror, like film stars have, and it's got a well posh kitchen. But I've been told not to cook if I don't want to 'cos Maureen can cook whatever I want and get one of the butlers to bring it up. HA HA HA HA! Oh and my apartment has a balcony that you can walk out on to, which looks out over green fields.

When Maureen went, I ran about for a while getting very excited opening cupboards and flicking the TV channels and jumping up and down on the bed and finding out what all the switches do on the walls and in the shower. It was weird 'cos I kept waiting for Cava-Sue and Murphy to run in and start trying to bagsy the bed or tell me to give them a go with the channel-flicker, or put something I didn't want to hear on the stereo. But obviously no one did.

So I unpacked the brand new MacBook Air that was lying on my bed in a box with a label that said 'Shiraz Bailey Wood: Personal Assistant', and messed about with it for a bit, and now I'm off to my bed, which has pure Egyptian cotton sheets from the Tiffany Poole Sleepeazzzy Bedlinen Range. I need to get some sleep. My head is proper mangled. I hope it all makes more sense tomorrow.

WEDNESDAY 4TH JANUARY

Well, today was another brainbender. Things at Mandalay Manor are getting more confusing, not clearer at all.

I got woken up proper abruptly at 7am this morning 'cos there was a camera crew at the end of my bed. One person was actually sitting on my feet, pointing a camera right in my face, while Karen was asking me questions. This wasn't exactly a flattering shot of me because my face was all in its just woken up state all crinkly like an old crisp-bag and I didn't have any lip-gloss or my gold hoops on or anything. I don't really want to be on telly looking like a minger.

'Good morning, Shiraz!' said Karen. 'We just thought we'd grab some footage of how you feel about being at Mandalay Manor! Like how you feel right now at this minute!' Well the truth was I didn't feel much really. I felt like my breath must smell 'cos I'd eaten an entire packet of Peanut M & Ms and not cleaned my teeth before bed.

I missed our Penny being cuddled up in bed with me like a magic ever-snoring hot water bottle. I also felt like I needed a wee. That was about it.

'Erm, I don't feel like anything really,' I said. Well Karen didn't look very happy when I said that so I said, 'Well I feel like this is the start of a very long journey! I don't know what this day's going to throw at me but I'm going to give it one hundred and ten per cent!'

Well this made Karen much happier and the film crew all went away then and let me get dressed in peace 'cos I only had a pair of knickers on and was sitting with a duvet up to my chin so no one could see my bits!

Soon after that I was called down to the sitting room to meet Tiffany Poole and film my first day of being a personal assistant. So I put on my red hoodie and jeans and some trainers and took a deep breath and set off downstairs to the main sitting room.

Well, when I reached the sitting-room doors, Karen took me to one side and said, 'OK, just to warn you, Tiffany looks a bit, erm, weird at the moment so we'll just be filming your top halves right? But just act normal and it'll make things a lot easier.'

'OK,' I said, feeling a bit scared really. What did she mean, weird? So I walked into the sitting room, alone at first as they were still setting the cameras up, and there was Tiffany Poole, standing in the bay windows. She was talking on her mobile phone. She gave me a quick thumbs-up to say hello, then carried on nattering.

Tiffany was dressed quite casual compared to how glam she normally is. She was wearing a little white vest top and some big baggy combat pants and a pair of big dark glasses. That's when I noticed she was leaning on a walking stick!

'Oh it's a right old mess, it's trickling everywhere, I can't wear anything tight, it's vile,' Tiffany was saying. 'That's the last time I use that surgeon! I mean the eyes look good, the forehead is good, but the rest is nasty. Anyway Olivia, do come home at some point. It would be good to catch up about Christmas. Tell Kitten 'well done' about the *Vogue* Teen party pictures. You're both all over the papers. You both look amazing. Got to go now, I'm filming something.'

Then she put the phone down, hobbled over to the sofa and said, 'Shiraz Bailey Wood! Good morning!'

Well I tried to act normal like Karen told me but I couldn't help myself, I had to say what I was thinking.

'What happened to you?' I said, 'Did you have an accident at your retreat!?' I said.

'Oooh ... erm ... hang on a minute,' said Tiffany, shouting to Karen who'd just walked in. 'What has Shiraz signed?! Has she signed the secrecy documents!?'

'Not yet,' said Karen, pushing a pile of paperwork as long as a novel underneath my nose. 'Shiraz? Can you just sign this please? It basically just says you won't tell the newspapers anything you hear or see here. Is that OK?'

I didn't know what to do. I didn't want to sign any

more of these stupid reality TV forms, but I didn't want anyone to think I'd be snidey or go blabbing stuff. 'Cos you don't do that to people, do you? It ain't nice. You don't tell people's secrets.

'I don't want any more scandal about me all over the newspapers, Shiraz!' said Tiffany. 'Those newspaper people are scum! They're obsessed with me! They're always poking their nose in where it's not wanted. I hate them!'

I felt bad then, so I signed the papers and gave them back to Karen.

Then Tiffany said, 'OK, so I haven't had an accident. I was having some work done over Christmas and the liposuction on my bum and thighs hasn't really stopped swelling yet.'

'Oh, right,' I said, feeling a bit queasy.

'Don't look so horrified, darling,' said Tiffany. 'I always get work done at Christmas. It's the only time I get free to do it. Usually, it works out fine, but, the lipo on the leg hasn't turned out so great this time. They jab a pipe in, you see? Then they suck out the fat. But my right thigh is a bit infected I think, it's sort of oozing puss now.'

Well my face went green just thinking about it.

'But on the upside,' said Tiffany. 'I had my eye bags removed, my lips plumped and some Botox on my forehead and that's been a complete success. What do you think?!'

She raised her sunglasses and showed me her face.

She looked as beautiful as ever, but a bit like someone had given her a few thumps around the face.

'I can cover this with makeup,' she said. 'It'll be gone in a few days. Good, eh?'

'It's, erm, great,' I said trying to sound like I meant it. To be honest, it made me feel quite sad. I was thinking about what a nice Christmas I'd just had with all my family, even if we did do each other's heads in a bit. Fancy spending all Christmas in hospital alone and coming back on a walking stick? All around us people were fiddling about with cameras and lighting, so I made my voice really quiet.

'Tiffany,' I said. 'Why did you have liposuction on your bum and thighs?! You're proper skinny.'

'Oh, darling, I wasn't before Christmas,' she said. 'I was a whale. That suit I had on when we filmed at your house was a UK size six! That's as big as a house!'

I didn't say anything when she said that. Size six is teeny weeny. I've argued this enough times with Carrie.

'But what about your Tiffany Poole Wellness Pills? They're meant to be good for staying slim aren't they? Don't they stop the body absorbing fat or something? And all that yoga you do too? I know someone who bought your Astanga yoga DVD when it came out. She said it was proper difficult and it gave her sore legs afterwards, so she only did it once.'

Tiffany looked proper confused when I said that. Like the Wellness Pills and the yoga didn't really register with her. Then she sort of laughed like she remembered, and then winced, although laughing made her hurt.

'Well it's a tough business this beauty thing, Shiraz,' she said. 'No pain, no gain.'

'Right, Shiraz, Tiffany, shall we get down to business?' shouted Karen. 'We're going to film all the opening shots for Episode One this morning. That will be you, Shiraz seeing your apartment, and Tiffany welcoming you to Mandalay Manor. Now don't worry, Shiraz, I've sent Sadie the researcher to pack all your things up into your suitcase so it looks like you're just arriving for the first time!'

'Hang on! You've done what?!' I said. I didn't want anyone fiddling about with my knickers and bras and things!

'Oh it's just to save time, don't worry.' Karen said. I felt pretty annoyed then but I counted slowly from one to ten in my head, 'cos I didn't want to kick off. That was just quite annoying. So was filming me with no makeup on at 7am!

'And, Shiraz, this afternoon,' Karen said, 'we're going to film some shots of Tiffany meeting some friends for lunch in London. We're going to drive down to a restaurant called The Wolseley in Piccadilly and meet up with some of Tiffany's girlfriends, and film Tiffany chatting and laughing about her new bikini range which you're all very very excited about!'

'Oh, I forgot about that,' tutted Tiffany. 'Who's coming by the way?'

'Erm, let me see,' said Karen checking her notes. 'Right, Cynthia Newton, Sophia Walden and Saffron Young.'

'Ughh, I can't stand any of them,' hissed Tiffany. 'Why are they in episode one? What have they got to do with my new bikini range?'

'Erm,' said Karen checking her notes. 'Well Cynthia is very "in" right now as she's just been made "face of L'Oreal", so your manager has said yes to that. Oh and Sophia is very big with *Heat* magazine readers, so that will mean you'll get a lot of publicity from them. You're going to be bridesmaid at Sophia's wedding, remember!? Oh, and Saffron was the only other person available and she's got a cookery book coming out she wants to promote!'

'OK,' Tiffany sighed. 'Fine. No problem.'

Well, this was getting a bit mental. Why was Tiffany meeting people she didn't even like? And why was Tiffany calling the first day of my new job 'the Bikini Episode'? I thought this show was about me being a personal assistant and my 'journey'.

'Are Cynthia and that lot not your real friends!?' I said to her. This was really bizarre. I've seen photos of these people in *OK* magazine, sitting round the table at Mandalay Manor, eating Tiffany's special roast leg of lamb dinners! They couldn't all be fake could they?

'Good heavens, no way. I can't bloody stand them,' laughed Tiffany.

'So, who are your real friends?!' I said to her.

'Well it depends on what you mean by "friends",
doesn't it, I suppose?' she said to me.

What a mental thing to say!

'Well, I mean your friends!' I said. 'Your bessie mates!
People who come round your house and just slob out and
watch telly and have a laugh with you? And who do you
go to Vue cinema and eat jelly snails with? Or if you have
an argument with your bloke, who do you call and have a
moan to? Y'know that type of friend!? Proper friends!'

'Oh, I see what you mean,' she said. 'Well . . . no one.
Not these days. Anyone I thought was a good friend
ended up selling stories about me to the papers and
buying themselves a new car or kitchen. I just keep
myself to myself. It's the best way. I mean, I know
thousands of people, but I don't think of any of them as
my friends.'

'Oh,' I said. I suddenly thought about Carrie and I
really missed her. 'Cos when we're not arguing we're
amazing friends. And Uma and Kezia, they're always
there for me too. They don't just hang about with me 'cos
they've got something to promote!

'Anyway, Shiraz,' Tiffany went on. 'I've thought of a
job for my new personal assistant to be getting on with.'

Tiffany picked up her mobile phone and wrote down
a mobile phone number on a sheet of Tiffany Poole 'PS
– I LOVE YOU' special embossed notepaper.

'This is my friend Darren,' Tiffany said. 'Can you call
him and say that Tiffany and her girlfriends are all going

to be having afternoon tea at The Wolseley in three hours if he wants to join us?'

'Oh, OK,' I laughed, 'Is this another one of your friends that you don't like?'

'Ooh, no,' she said. 'Darren works for a paparazzi agency. He'll send someone down to take some nice long-lens photos of the whole thing to sell to the newspapers tomorrow. At least then I'll get half the money.'

I couldn't believe what I was hearing.

'But I thought you hated the newspapers and the paparazzi?' I said.

'Yeah, but this is different, Shiraz,' Tiffany said to me, 'This is business.'

TUESDAY 9TH JANUARY

I'm settling in a bit more at Mandalay Manor now.

It was all proper scary at first, but I'm beginning to understand Tiffany's 'famous' world a bit better now. All this A-List celebrity stuff, having stacks of money, being a well-known face etc. It's totally different to just being normal Shiraz Bailey Wood. It's a complete other planet, a billion miles away from Thundersley Road.

Since I got to Mandalay Manor, I don't think I've ever touched real money. I've been given a special Tiffany Poole business chargecard that I can use to pay for stuff I need. But I don't NEED anything. The house is full of food and Tiffany gets sent bags and bags of free makeup and amazing beauty products all day long. People just send her free things and hope she'll have her photo taken holding it. She doesn't even look at most of it. It all just stacks up in a room, like a big lip-gloss mountain. Carrie would faint if she saw it. Then she'd try and climb it while trying them all on!

I took the chargecard to the village shop the other day just to see if it worked. It did! I bought a box of Tampax, a *Glamour* magazine and a massive bar of Cadbury's Fruit and Nut. Afterwards, I sat outside the shop on a bench remembering all of the times me and Cava-Sue have stuck our hands down the back of the couch finding change to buy nappies. I wonder if having money feels like this when it's yours? Do you ever feel happy or do you just feel a bit guilty and weird?

My main worry last week was that this *Help Me I'm a Celebrity!* job was totally fake and Tiffany didn't really need an assistant. But the fact is that she totally needs an assistant. Tiffany needs someone to be around her, just sort of being with her and listening to her, 'cos she can't cope with stuff on her own. It's like being famous has made her into a little girl or something. She's not good at working out what she might need for a day out or finding her own house keys or putting on her shoes when she's talking on the phone or anything like that. She needs someone to do it for her. And it's not like she's got her mum to give her a hand 'cos Tiffany is in the middle of a big multi-million pound legal dispute with her own mum so they're not speaking! Imagine suing your own mother!? OH MY DAYZ!!

I said to Tiffany yesterday, ' 'Ere Tiffany, that's a bit tight, innit? It's your own mother! It's your own flesh and blood! Can't you just take her down Toby Tavern and both have a carvery together and have a laugh about things?'

That's what my sister Cava-Sue does when she rows with my mother! They're down there once a month! In fact I reckon my mother just starts arguments now 'cos she fancies some sticky toffee pudding with an everlasting refillable jug of custard!'

Well Tiffany shrugged when I said that. 'It's all a lot more serious than that, Shiraz. That woman sold all the photos of me as a baby for two million dollars to somebody who was writing a horrible book about me! How could my mother do that?! How?!'

'Y'know something, Tiffany?' I said. 'I dunno. I reckon mothers just make mistakes sometimes. Like when my mother used to cut mine and our Cava-Sue's hair with kitchen scissors every time it was school photo day. Well in fairness we should have sued her for that but we didn't. We had to forgive her for that eventually, 'cos she's our mother. You only get one mum, Tiffany, innit.'

I don't think Tiffany was listening to that last bit. Tiffany's got a proper short span of concentration. You have to say stuff to her in tiny little sentences or her head just drifts thinking about what to wear for that night's awards ceremony red carpet. To be honest, when you're talking to Tiffany Poole, it's best if you keep the conversation all about Tiffany, 'cos she's not used to chatting about other people's lives at all.

For example, if you say to her, 'How's it going today Tiffany?!' She'll give you a big long answer that takes up about ten minutes. But don't ever ever expect her to say, 'Oh and how about you, Shiraz? How are you?' It's like all Tiffany Poole is used to doing now is being interviewed by reporters who want to know about her life, so she's totally forgotten about how a normal two-way conversation works!!

OH MY LIFE, even Kezia knows how a normal conversation works! Even if Kez does suck her teeth right in the middle of you speaking and shout 'GOODMAYES GIRL RUN TING, SHIIZZLE BIZZLE, AIGHT!?' Oh my dayz, I miss Kezia a lot. I texted her today and said, 'How iz you? xxx' and she sent me a text right back that said, 'Fat – Like a kid Who Likes Cake Innit, Blad, Want This Baby Out Now!! Miss You Shizza, Kez, xx'.

I felt well homesick for a bit then, but I put it out of my mind 'cos Tiffany needed me to call her beautician and book an emergency blackhead extraction for her. I told Tiffany I'd steam her head over the kettle then squeeze it myself like I do Murphy's but Tiffany said, thank you Shiraz but she'd rather consult a professional.

* * *

WEDNESDAY 10TH JANUARY

Today was a sort of typical day at Mandalay Manor. Well as typical as days get here anyway.

I woke up at about seven when I heard the sound of a van coming down the drive bringing today's newspapers. Tiffany Poole has all of the newspapers delivered every day to her front door. She gets *The Sun, The Mirror, The Star* and *The Daily Mail,* plus all of the big posh heavy newspapers too.

The second I hear the van I run down the stairs to the letterbox before Tiffany wakes up and grab them. Then me and Maureen lay them all out in the downstairs staff kitchen on the big oak table and we go through them page by page finding anything at all about Tiffany Poole, reading it and working out whether to hide it from Tiffany or not. I thought this was well weird at first but Maureen assures me this makes the day ahead a lot easier.

Like I say there's a picture of Tiffany walking up a red carpet into the new *Spiderman* premiere looking all beautiful and slim, well we don't hide that. We show her that. That's good. However, just say someone's taken a photo of her with her eyes a bit wonky or a bogey in her nose or her arms looking even slightly wide like she might have a hint of bingo-wing? Well then we rip the page out and put it right into the shredder!

We make sure the film crew never know about this either 'cos Tiffany tells people she doesn't care what people say about her in the papers. Tiffany says it's nothing to her because she's heard it all before. She says it's 'water off a duck's back' and she's not in the tiniest bit bothered. But I don't believe Tiffany when she says that now because sometimes she seems proper upset and angry. And OH MY DAYZ I would GO MENTAL SCHIZOID BALLISTIC if anyone said some of this stuff about me or my family! 'Cos the newspapers just make up stuff that is total rubbish!

Like this week, Tiffany went out in a dress that she'd worn once before a few years ago, so a newspaper said that must be 'cos she's nearly skint and can't afford any new dresses! That's not true at all! She just liked that dress! It cost three grand!

And then another night she went to a restaurant and ate a tiny bowl of pasta which is a LOT for Tiffany. Well on her way back to her car someone took a photo of her with her belly sticking out a bit with food in it, then they put it on the front of the newspaper with the headline 'TIFFANY POOLE – PREGNANT AGAIN?' And then a few days later, after Tiffany had been all paranoid about her figure and starving herself again and Maureen was nagging her to bloody eat, the newspaper ran some before and after pictures and wrote: 'TIFFANY POOLE – LOSES BABY?!' But there weren't ever a baby in the first place! It was all just made up. And obviously, I'd feel more flipping sorry for Tiffany about all this if I didn't know that when it suits her, she rings the newspapers herself and arranges for them to pop up and take 'surprise' photos of her!

Because the crazy mentaloid thing is that when Tiffany Poole's face is all over the papers it make her sad, but when she's not in the newspapers at all, well that makes her even sadder! Her head is in a well funny place, I reckon. She can't win, can she? I feel terrible writing this but I hope Carrie Draper never ever gets to be this famous. Sometimes famous don't seem like much fun at all.

Today me and Maureen put a whole page into the shredder that was from *The Daily Mail* by this horrid lady who had written a big long 'opinion column' quacking on for about two thousand bloody words about Tiffany!

The woman was getting proper irate saying that Tiffany has no control over her daughter Olivia, and it's rumoured that Olivia lives mainly in London now and is running wild with the socialite Kitten Montague-Jones and the 'London party-crowd'. Oh, and Tiffany doesn't care about her other children anyway, they're brought up by nannies. And Tiffany's husband Peter Flazio spends more time in their London apartment hanging out with his 'close male friends' than in the family home! And Tiffany is even taking her poor little defenceless mother to court! And while children in Africa starve, Tiffany spends money like water!

According to this journalist lady, Tiffany Poole is OLD AND PAST IT and her plastic surgery is fooling no one!

'*Look at her hands! She has hands like old claws! She says she's thirty-four, but she's must be at least forty-five!*' In fact this journalist who was writing the column reckoned she knew people personally who knew Tiffany Poole personally and they say FOR SURE that Tiffany is horrible and manipulative and boring! In fact Tiffany Poole represents everything that is bad and wrong and evil about Great Britain today and she must be stopped!

To be honest, the woman writing the article sounded a bit mental and proper jealous.

'I don't think Tiffany needs to see that one does she, Shiraz?' Maureen said to me when we read it. Then we stuck the entire copy of *The Daily Mail* into the shredder and emptied all the bits into the recycling box and had some cups of coffee and homemade bread toast and jam. Maureen's bread is gorgeous and the jam is from the farm next door.

Afterwards we made Tiffany her morning breakfast tray of an egg-white omelette and a glass of sparkling mineral water and a spinach salad with the oil dressing on the side, then we took it up to her room and woke her up. I felt sad as we were walking up the stairs 'cos it's not like Tiffany is an angel or nothing but she's not anywhere near as terrible as that woman was making out. In fact her life is a little bit boring really. She never does anything proper crazy. All she does is lots of photo-shoots, try on clothes, watch a bit of telly with her kids, and work out which bit of her body needs to be swapped or chopped off. Me and Carrie used to act miles naughtier than Tiffany Poole.

It's weird though, 'cos everyone in Britain thinks they know exactly what Tiffany Poole is like and that they can say whatever they like about her 'cos she's not a real person and it won't hurt her feelings. I don't think Carrie could cope with being famous at all. Carrie cried for three days when someone wrote 'Carrie Draper is an ugly slut' on the comment section of her Bebo. She was gutted beyond belief.

I rang my Wesley today and told him about the paper shredder and the egg-white omelette. I can't tell him much else though 'cos I've signed an official secrecy document so everything has to stay hush hush.

Wesley was well narked when I said that. 'But it's bloody me, Shiraz! I'm your boyfriend, innit!' he moaned at me.

So I said to him, 'Look Wes I'd rather not tell you anything 'cos maybe you'll forget and slip up and tell someone and the thing is you can't trust no one.'

I asked Wes how Bezzie was doing and Wesley thought for a second and he said, 'Well actually, Shiraz, Bezzie's life is looking up a bit at the moment, but I've promised him I won't tell anyone so I can't tell you nothing, innit.'

'What do you mean?' I said. 'How's it's looking up!? Has he got a woman?'

'I'm sorry, Shiraz,' he said, 'But it's a secret. If I tell you then it might slip out. You can't trust no one can you, innit?'

'Oh, whatever, Wesley Barrington Bains II,' I said, giggling. 'Fair enough. Look, love you, gotta go, text you later.'

But after I put the phone down I thought about what a proper weird thing I'd just said to my Wesley. 'You can't trust no one.' OH MY DAYZ! Of course you can trust people! It's just Tiffany Poole that can't really trust people! I ain't famous! I don't need to be all paranoid like her.

THURSDAY 11TH JANUARY

This afternoon Karen and the film crew came over to do some filming for episode three of *Tiffany Poole: Help Me I'm a Celebrity!*. Today they wanted footage of Tiffany popping down to a bikini factory in West London to deliver some more of her fresh designs for her new Tiffany Poole: Atlantis bikini range.

So I packed Tiffany's handbag and told her how cold it was so she'd need a jacket, and after about an hour of fussing we set off.

As we were getting into the limo, I asked Tiffany if she had her designs with her but she just started laughing and said, 'No, don't worry, Shiraz, we'll do some on the way down there.' I thought this was a bit odd. So we set off and as the car crawled through Surrey towards west London Tiffany got out a pen and paper out of her bag and drew a few squiggles on a page. She drew some women's bodies and then she drew some bikinis on them. Then she said, 'Shiraz, what colour bikini do you think my fans want to wear?'

Immediately I thought of Carrie. 'Pink?' I said.

So Tiffany drew an arrow to the bikini and wrote 'PINK' in big letters. Then she drew a few more squiggly women and drew spots and stars on them and said, 'OK, that's that done,' and put the 'designs' back in her bag.

'Is that how you design bikinis?!' I said. I think my mouth was wide open with shock!

'Oh, that's not the full design. The designers do the designing!' she said.

'So what was that then?!' I said.

'Oh, that's just my thoughts and vibes for the designers to, y'know, play with. I just bring my personality to the collection. I don't actually design anything.'

Well I didn't know what to think. I know that Carrie buys those bikinis and they're fifty-odd quid each, and she totally thinks that Tiffany stays up all night slaving away designing them. It seemed a bit of a con.

So we got to the factory and the film crew filmed me and Tiffany walking through the front doors and going up to the offices to meet the manager.

There were about two hundred fans all waiting at the factory gates to see Tiffany. People were crying and screaming and trying to get through the mesh fence to touch her. It's quite scary really. Some of the people

185

didn't look right in the head to me. I don't know how Tiffany puts up with that every day of her life, every single time she leaves Mandalay Manor. She has to take this bloke called Carlos, a massive security guy, with her every where she goes.

So we ran inside and then Tiffany changed into a bikini and walked about the offices giving the staff a 'first glimpse' of the new range being modelled by the designer. This was mostly for the cameras to be honest. It was just an excuse for Tiffany to show her new bone-thin size zero body off to the cameras, now that all her liposuction scars have stopped bleeding and dripping.

After that they filmed me running around after Tiffany helping her to hold up these massive, professional-looking A4 size sheets of bikini designs that she'd been 'working on herself' all of the night before! OH MY DAYZ HOW FAKE IS THAT!?

All the factory staff clapped and told Tiffany how mega-talented she was and then the director shouted 'Cut! Thank you! That's episode three finished!'

Finally we drove back to Mandalay Manor and I went upstairs and sat in my apartment on my own and I wanted to speak to my family, but Murph picked up and said that Mum and Cava-Sue were down the bingo and he couldn't speak 'cos he was playing *Grand Theft Auto* with Lewis and his pizza was burning under the grill. CHEERS, MURPHY!

So I put the phone down and realised how totally

silent my apartment and the whole of Mandalay Manor was. And for the first time I bloody missed the noise and the smell and the realness of Thundersley Road and Goodmayes and Essex.

MONDAY 15TH JANUARY

We didn't do any filming today. Tiffany had an important appointment with Byron Brown, her business manager. It was at a mega posh restaurant in London called Claridges. I didn't think I was invited but Tiffany asked me if I wouldn't mind tagging along. She does that a lot these days. I'm not sure why. I think that sometimes she just feels proper lonely and the fact is I make her laugh.

'You have a good way of looking at things, Shiraz!' she said to me this morning when I was passing her four teaspoons of low-carb fibre pellets and some flax seeds in a bowl with skimmed milk. 'The thing with you, Shiraz, is you always tell me the truth!'

Well I felt guilty when Tiffany said that 'cos, yes, fair enough, I am one of the most honest people around her but I don't always tell her the truth. In fact I'd only just finished putting a two-page article from *The Mirror*, which was calling her house decor and her garden tastes 'common and nasty', through the paper shredder.

I suppose the thing about me and Tiffany is that I don't go crawling round her telling her she's right all the time, like her staff and her public relations people and her managers do. Like this morning I told her straight to her face she was a mentalist to consider having one of her ears actually surgically cut off and sewn back on again 'less wonky'.

'Tiffany,' I said, 'I'm telling you straight, bruv, this is madness! This is actual solid-gold-LOONY-ON-THE-LOOSE-QUICK-POLICE-WE'VE-GOT-HER-mentalism!' Then I told her that if she mentioned it again I was going to ring her doctor up on Harley Street in London and get him to drive round and sedate her. Well Tiffany laughed the most I've ever seen her laugh ever when I said that. It was nice to see her laugh. She looked proper pretty. She wouldn't need all this makeup and stylists if she just smiled more and looked happy.

Then I said, 'Anyway, who said your ear was wonky?!' and Tiffany said 'Oh I was speaking yesterday with Genevieve Shaw. Y'know, Genevieve who presents *Supermodel Unmasked*? She's trying to fix up a date for dinner. She wants to bring a film crew to Mandalay Manor to do some filming to promote her new series. Oh and she was mentioning she had a great surgeon to get my ear sorted out if I wanted.'

Well I nearly spat my coffee all over the sitting room floor when Tiffany said that. 'I don't like that woman,' I said to Tiffany. 'I think she's horrible. Sorry Tiffany, but that's how I feel. I'm only keeping it real.'

'Oh, don't worry,' said Tiffany. 'I can't stand her either.'

The trip to Claridges was proper interesting. Well, if you're a nosybonk like I am. And it had a very interesting result too. Tiffany was meeting Byron to have a chat about the financial state of Tiffany Poole Incorporated now that Christmas was over and everyone in Britain had done their Christmas shopping and bought all her different products. And OH MY DAYZ it's safe to say that it was good news and Tiffany ain't going to be down Lidl buying six-pence cans of Latvian baked beans or cut-price salami that looks like old man's todger any day soon. Not likely! No, Tiffany Poole will be rich beyond her wildest dreams forever. My eyes were spinning as Byron started talking Tiffany through the figures.

'So, Tiffany,' Byron said. 'The biggest hit this Christmas was your personally designed homeware selection! The pans, the plates, the gravy boats, bed linen etc!'

'Crikey,' said Tiffany, looking surprised. 'Some of that was a right old load of overpriced rubbish. Forty-seven pounds for a gravy boat? Who bought that?!'

'Forty-seven thousand people bought the gravy boat!' laughed Byron. 'Everyone wants a home life like Tiffany Poole! Also, we've already had seven-hundred-and-fifty-thousand pounds' worth of pre-orders for your Tiffany Poole Atlantis bikini range!'

'The ones you don't even bloody design, Tiffany!' I felt like shouting. But I bit my lip and sat on my hands.

'Now, sales of your perfume Gush have been amazing!

And from Boxing Day onwards,' Byron continued, 'every female in Britain has been trying to lose their post-Christmas extra fat, so sales of your yoga DVD and Wellness Pills have gone through the roof! The shelves are literally empty! They're all trying to get a body like you, Tiffany!'

'Pghhghgh! They'll be bloody lucky,' I tutted. But this time I didn't think it, I actually said it out loud!

'What did you say, Shiraz?!' Tiffany said.

'I said, they'll be bloody lucky, Tiffany! You don't do yoga or take Wellness Pills! You live on egg-white omelettes and have all the fat sucked out your bum with a pipe once every six months. I've never seen you do so much as one single star jump ever!'

Well there was a deathly silence. And then Tiffany and Byron burst out laughing.

'I like her!' Byron said to Tiffany pointing at me. 'You should keep hold of this one!

'I know,' laughed Tiffany and then they just carried on chatting.

I wasn't finding this whole conversation bare jokes though. It was making me proper irate. I couldn't stop thinking about Carrie and all the other millions of girls in Britain spending all this money chasing a dream that don't really exist.

'Cos it don't exist, does it?! It ain't real.

Tiffany Poole's life, the bits we're all buying and trying to copy – it's all fake. She don't eat steak and kidney puddings all day and still stay naturally size zero with huge big boobs. She don't have big perfect parties with all her perfect friends round where she cooks perfect food with her perfect pans and perfect plates and serves gravy in a perfect silver gravy boat. She isn't actually a talented bikini designer, or a brilliant author. It's all a sham. In fact the only thing that's real and for sure is that Tiffany Poole is proper unbelievably rich and famous and that don't seem to make her that happy. And ever since Carrie has been obsessed with being like her I don't think she's been happy either.

'Now, Tiffany,' Byron said. 'Sales of your last novel *Forever Dream* by Tiffany Poole have been amazing! And I've got another offer I wanted to run by you.'

By this point I could tell Tiffany weren't listening properly, she'd drifted off again,

'My what?' said Tiffany,

'Your novels,' said Byron.. 'You've sold five hundred thousand this Christmas!'

'What was the last one about?' asked Tiffany, who was fidgeting in her seat now.

'Erm,' said Byron reading his notes. 'It was about a famous model who finds love with a footballer and they buy a mansion.'

'Oh yeah, I remember now,' Tiffany said. 'So the girl who wrote it did a good job then?!'

'Not bad!' said Byron. 'The publishing house are thrilled! In fact they're wondering if you'd like to write a children's book next!'

Tiffany just laughed when he said that.

'Byron, I didn't write my adult books,' she sighed, 'How can I write for kids!?'

'Oh we'll do the same as last time,' he said. 'We'll give someone some of your thoughts and vibes, then get them to do the rest! Just one little book! I'm sure you can do that. Thoughts and vibes!'

'I've got no thoughts and vibes left,' sighed Tiffany, looking at her watch in a bored manner, 'I've sold them all already!'

'She'll do it,' I said. It just burst out of my mouth somehow. 'I can help her a bit!'

I don't know why I said that. It's just that I love writing stuff. And I know all about telling kids stories! I'm Essex's best babysitter!

Tiffany just looked at me, then looked at Byron then said, 'OK then Byron, I'll have a think. Shiraz will send you something through as soon as possible. Now can I go please? I want to go to Garrards the jewellers and buy some new earrings. Genevieve Shaw is coming to my house for dinner soon. I need something that makes my ears look less wonky.

THURSDAY 18TH JANUARY

I scribbled down some ideas for Tiffany Poole's new children's book today and I mailed them to that Byron geezer. I don't think they were much good, but I had a giggle doing it. It reminded me of back in Year Eleven when I was in Ms Bracket's GCSE class. I used to write down all these funny little stories that made all the class wee themselves laughing. Ms Bracket was the only teacher who didn't just tell me off for it and say she'd put me in pupil referral unit. She could see I was just using my imagination. Ms Bracket used to say I had a proper talent with words, but I never knew how much she really meant it. I mean, fair enough, I was good at English compared to, say, Kezia Marshall. But the only thing thing Kezia ever read on a regular basis was the back of the morning-after pill packet and it turns out she weren't much good at reading that either, was she?

But I like writing though, even if I ain't that great at it. It makes my brain feel proper alive.

So I sat down on my bed to write this morning and I tried to think of a story that would be sort of about Tiffany Poole and capture her 'personality'. But nothing seemed to fit. I started writing one about a magic shrinking girl who gets smaller and smaller 'cos someone keeps putting a pipe in her thigh and sucking all her fat out, but, that didn't seem to be a very happy story. In fact if a little girl heard it, I reckon she might have nightmares. And the harder I tried to think, the more this other story kept jumping out of my head instead. The story was called *The Incredibly Pretty Princess*. It was about an incredibly pretty princess called Princess Caroline who had long blonde hair who lived in a castle with black iron gates and fountains. The Incredibly Pretty Princess was the prettiest girl in the whole of the kingdom. In fact, Princess Caroline was so totally pretty that passing princes and soldiers couldn't see or think straight when they caught a glimpse of her prettiness. In fact they would fall off their horses, or ride them into rivers and all that type of thing.

The Incredibly Pretty Princess had a royal dog called Alexandra who was also very, very pretty, but very, very silly, with a brain as tiny as a tiny flake of salt. The princess carried Alexandra everywhere in a basket made of woven gold and pink flowers. The Princess and her silly dog were proper bare jokes hilarious and got into all types of mentalist adventures. Like one day the Incredibly Pretty Princess and Alexandra went to the countryside to enjoy the sunshine and visit a magical lake. Well Princess Caroline got so distracted by the prettiness of her reflection in the water that when the sun went in she scooped up the wrong dog and took it home to the castle. But it wasn't a dog, it was a terrible, hideous growly wolf!

And another time the Incredibly Pretty Princess had an amazing adventure when a terrible storm hit the castle and all her maids and guards had to run for the hills to survive. But the Incredibly Pretty Princess is so pretty and her beauty sleep is so very deep that she slept right through everyone calling! And when she woke up she'd been blown to another land completely!

Well anyway, I scribbled some of this down and

emailed it off. I suppose it was a bit of a waste of time really now I think about it. In fact the one thing that's come out of today for some weird reason is that I can't stop thinking how much I miss Carrie Draper. I don't know why I keep thinking of her. It's not like I've had any spare time today or anything, 'cos as I say, I've been writing a book.

SATURDAY 28TH JANUARY

OH MY DAYZ! Y'know how I said that we never listen to our Murphy much 'cos he usually talks rubbish. Well he totally had a point when he said Shiraz Bailey Wood's life should be made into a movie! And no, not a horror movie either! A proper exciting movie that people of all ages and sizes and colours and religions could join together as one at Vue cinema to see, and eat jelly snails, and laugh till their knickers actually dissolved into the velvet seats with all the seas of widdle.

My life would be a movie so BARE JOKES, that say you'd gone down to Vue to watch another movie, and the trailer for my movie came on, you would NEVER be all sarcastic and say, 'Ooh we must get tickets for this', 'cos you would really mean it and you'd be there on the first night with your hotdog and your Häagen Dazs proper dying for it to begin! 'Cos that's how exciting yesterday and last night was like. I'm going to write it all down so I'll never forget.

I woke up yesterday morning at seven in my bedroom at Mandalay Mansion and the first thing I remembered was the massive big dinner party happening there tonight. Tiffany Poole and her husband Peter Flazio were hosting a special dinner for Genevieve Shaw, to celebrate the start of *Supermodel Unmasked*. Now just the thought of this was giving me the bumshudders. I don't know why 'cos it's not like I had to sit and eat with Genevieve Shaw and that prat with the hat François or the woman with the dark glasses, 'cos I wasn't even going to the dinner. No, I ain't allowed near the other celebrities now on account of my 'keeping it real' policy which tends to offend them. Like the other day one of Tiffany's 'friends' was wondering out loud whether five grand was too much to spend on a handbag.

I said, 'No, not at all, as long as you blank out of your head the idea of African babies covered in flies waiting for someone to give five grand that would feed their entire village for a year and stop them all carking it!'

And then the room went very silent and Tiffany said I didn't need to do any more assisting today.

But just the thought of Genevieve Shaw coming to Mandalay Manor was making me feel all tense. After what she said to Carrie. I kept thinking about all those girls who went to the O2 Arena that day and how many of them must have left in a proper state and started wanting their faces re-set or gone on stupid diets, or got told they walked funny or had funny ears or had eyes too close or too wide apart or just basically weren't good enough.

I started thinking of all sorts of ways to get revenge on the evil old bat. First I thought about cling-filming the guest toilet seats. No, too messy. Putting fart powder in the dinner? Oh what's the point? No one that Tiffany knows ever eats anything, they just live on fresh air and laxatives and that's why their breath smells like old sewage tank when you get up close to them.

I thought that maybe I could go up to her and point out what I think she could change about herself! But that would make me as bad as her. I even thought about just walking up and giving her a swift smack across the chops. But then I remembered my promise to Uma. Violence is never the answer.

So I hung about the house for a while watching Maureen dusting down the table and polishing the solid silver gravy boat and setting all the table places. And then camera crews began arriving to film some scenes of Genevieve hanging out with her great friend Tiffany for *Supermodel Unmasked*. And the film crew from *Tiffany Poole: Help Me I'm a Celebrity!* turned up to film some scenes of Tiffany 'chillaxing' with her close personal showbiz best mate, Genevieve Shaw. And in the middle of all this fuss Tiffany's husband Peter made a rare appearance in the driveway in his Jaguar accompanied by his film crew shooting footage for his new reality TV series called *The Beautiful Game: Peter Flazio Uncovered*, where Peter basically drives about in a car all day and goes to football practice and buys expensive shirts for fourteen episodes and, honest to God, it's the most boring reality TV show ever. Even the stuff they fake is boring. Well by six o'clock the house was full to the brim with camera crews and I was starting to feel quite hacked off.

Then I heard the unmistakable sound of Genevieve Shaw's angry crow voice in the hallway, saying 'Oh wow! What an amaaaaaaaazing home you have!' so I turned on my heel and ran off.

I went to my bedroom and flipped open my MacBook Air and checked if Wesley or Uma or Cava-Sue was around on MSN, but no one was online.

Then I faffed about on Bebo. I looked at Carrie's page for a while being proper nosy. I saw she'd changed her relationship status to 'in a relationship'.

I didn't know whether to feel sad or happy. It felt weird not knowing who it was. I just hoped someone nice was looking after her. Someone a bit decent who realised how special she was.

And that's when a message popped up in my email inbox. It was from Byron Brown, Tiffany's manager. He had an idea to put to me and he wanted me to ring him. So I phoned Byron right away and he said to me that he'd read Tiffany's vibes and feelings about the Incredibly Pretty Princess idea and he really liked the concept a lot. So did the publishing house. They wanted to get someone to write them into proper books and publish them in the new Tiffany Poole: Bedtime Stories range.

'Oh amazing!' I said, feeling proper proud, 'I liked them too! I'll tell Tiffany after dinner! Wow!'

'It's funny though isn't it?' said Byron, 'Because Tiffany was saying she was totally cleaned out of vibes and feelings. But then she had a burst of inspiration like this! Now that is odd isn't it?'

Well I just laughed. I wasn't going to grass Tiffany up and say she didn't even know I'd sent them. It didn't seem fair. Tiffany is nice really. Famous, but nice.

'And the thing is, I was wondering if she'd maybe had a bit of help with *The Incredibly Pretty Princess*?' said Byron. 'Because if so, there's a small sum of money I'd like to pay to the creator for the idea.'

'How much money?!' I said.

'Eight thousand pounds,' he said. 'In fact I could transfer the cash into their bank account almost immediately.'

Well I didn't say anything to that. I just sat there gobsmacked for three minutes and then Byron said, 'Shiraz Bailey Wood? Are you still on the line?!'

'Yeah,' I said. 'Course I am, I'm just proper amazed that's all.'

Byron laughed a bit and I started laughing too.

'So what will you do with the money, Shiraz?' he asked me.

Well I didn't even have to think about that. 'I'm going back to Essex and I'm going to college to do the rest of my A-Levels. Then I want to go to university. I'm planning to expand my brain to a terrifying level and take over the world, then other planets, then planets that ain't even been discovered yet!'

Byron roared with laughter when I said that. 'You sound very confident about that, Shiraz,' he said.

'Well, what can I say, Byron, bruv? I'm only keeping it real.'

I floated about the apartment in a cloud of happiness for about half an hour thinking about the money. Eight grand! That's more money that I can even imagine! The main thing I decided then and there is that I'm not going to tell anyone about it. Not my family, not Wesley, not anyone. This will be well hard 'cos I don't like keeping secrets but I know that if they all find out about it then it'll just make everything more complicated. I've got to find my own way here. Be the master of my own destiny and all that stuff. Eight grand could buy train fares to look at colleges and rent me a room somewhere and get me some books to study from and pay for one of those funny black cardboard hat things you wear when you get your degree and, OH MY DAYZ, my brain was well racing ahead of me!

Or was I just being selfish?! Should I give it to my mother instead to go on holiday? She's always moaning on that she's never been anywhere. Or should I give it to Cava-Sue to spend on Fin?

NO! I have to be strong here. I've got to go on my own journey! And yeah, I know the percentage don't exist but I believed it one hundred and ten per cent!

And in the middle of all the headrush my phone started bleeping with a text. I grabbed it and saw it was from Kezia. It said 'SHIZ! OH MY GOD! PLEASE COME! BABY COMING NOW! IN HOSPITAL! I'M ON MY OWN, BLUD COME AND HELP!'

Well the moment I saw that text, my heart started racing, big time. Kezia was more important than any of this.

I pulled on my hoodie and trainers, rang Tiffany's chauffeur and asked if he could do me a big, massive favour. 'I need to go to Essex right away!' I said. 'To Goodmayes, to the hospital! My friend is having a baby!'

'No problem, Miss Wood,' he said. 'I'll bring the limo round the front of the house immediately.'

I crept down the stairs and out of the front door. All I could hear was Genevieve talking loudly about her new show and everyone laughing.

'. . . Oh, the creatures that come along to the auditions!' Genevieve was howling. 'I don't know how they dare show their faces!'

No one even noticed me leaving.

The journey to Essex was well stressful. I called Kezia's mobile and she picked up but she was puffing and panting like crazy.

'Where's your mother!?' I shouted. 'Is she on her way too!?'

'I dunno!' Kezia said. 'She went down Mecca bingo and her phone's out of credit! If she has a win her mates sometimes go out drinking! Amira my next-door neighbour is looking after Tiq! My baby's come early Shiz! I'm scared rotten. This ain't like the last time. This is proper painful already ... aghghghghghghghgh ... bloody contraction, Shiz!'

'Where are you!?' I shouted. 'You're in bed right?'

'Nah. I'm on the wall outside the hospital! They won't let me use my mobile inside innit!' she shouted. Then she started crying. I don't think I've ever heard Kezia cry.

'Kezia,' I said, calmly, 'go back indoors, tell the nurse your contractions are proper bad now, get into bloody bed and I'll be on my way.'

I put the phone down and made a few phone calls trying to find Kez's mother. No one knew where she was.

I rang my Wesley and he said he'd meet me there.

Well I've never been so glad to see Goodmayes Hospital. And thank God Kezia wasn't still sitting on the wall when we arrived. There was a load of people there who'd pulled their chemotherapy drips out into the carpark to have a ciggie, but no Kez.

I thanked the limo driver with all my heart and told him he'd go to heaven for helping me and he laughed and said it was nice to use the car for something useful.

Then I ran up to the maternity ward. Well I could tell

from the screens that Kezia was in there and the baby thing was all systems go. So I ran to the front desk and said that I wanted to see Kezia Marshall and the midwife on duty smiled and said, 'Oh good, I'm glad someone has arrived who can support her. We had another visitor twenty minutes ago but she's not being very helpful!' The nurse pointed down the corridor, and that's when I saw Carrie Draper looking very, very unhappy. Her face was as white as a sheet! She was dressed in a green gown and white gloves and she was leaning against the wall sweating.

I ran up to her and said, 'Carrie! What's happening?!'

Well Carrie just looked at me and says, 'Oh my god, Shiraz, it's horrible! Horrible!'

'What's horrible?!' I said.

'Oh there's blood and stuff and goo and the baby's head is poking out and everything! I can't handle it, Shiraz!'

'Carrie Draper!' I gave her a bit of a poke. 'That's just having a baby! We've got to go in and support Kez! She ain't got no one else! Come on Carrie, it's going to be OK! Where do I get those gown things from!?' So I went and got myself a green gown and a mask and we crept into the room where Kez was lying, doing that mooing thing that Cava-Sue did when she gave birth to Fin. Kez was all covered in sweat and looking all mad when we walked in. She put out her hand when I saw her and I grabbed it and held it tight. Carrie was just staring now as the baby's head was poking right out of Kezia! And the hair on the baby's head was dark red. Red, like Clinton Brunton-Fletcher's!

'Now, nice strong pushes! We're nearly there,' said the midwife. 'Come on, Kezia, good girl! Push!'

'I am bloody pushing!' screamed Kezia. 'I can't push no more! Just get a suction thing now and pull it out! I bloody give up!'

'Don't give up, Kezia!' shouted Carrie. 'It's nearly there! Come on Kez, Goodmayes Girls Run Ting, innit!'

Well Kezia sort of laughed then and I laughed and Carrie laughed and then Kezia started screaming again and then she started puffing and panting like she'd just ran a marathon, and in the middle of a big long screeeeeam the baby just seemed to pop out!

It was a boy! And he was really big! He weren't like a tiny little weeny baby! He was like a big chunk with red hair and big powerful lungs and little scrunched fists and a cross face! He weighed ten pounds and one ounce!

'Oh my God! He is the most beautiful baby in the world!' sighed Kezia, cuddling him up into her chest. Me and Carrie stayed for a bit and then we tumbled out into the corridor, feeling proper proud. I think at some level we felt like *we*'d given birth to the baby.

And I couldn't believe what I saw when we got into the waiting room, because there was my Wesley Barrington Bains II and Bezzie Kelleher sitting there.

Bezzie stood up and gave Carrie a kiss on the forehead

and said, 'Well done, sweetheart, I told you you'd be good.'

Well I just looked at Wesley and he smiled at me and said, 'Oh yeah, they're back together, innit. I was going to tell you, but I didn't want everyone to know! I signed a secrecy thing, innit.'

'Wesley Barrington Bains II, how could you?!' I gasped. But I knew what he was getting at. Carrie and Bezzie looked really happy. She looked a lot healthier and he looked like he had something to live for again. You can't say fairer than that, can you?

I'm so glad me and Carrie are speaking again. We need to take things slowly and have a big proper chat, but I know stuff is going to be OK.

I took my mobile phone outside and called Uma Brunton-Fletcher and said I had something proper important that Kezia wanted me to tell her.

Lord alive, if they made this day into a Shiraz Bailey Wood movie, it would be proper non-stop action.

You'd never get time to eat your jelly snails ever.

TUESDAY 30TH JANUARY

I moved my stuff out of Mandalay Manor today. Well, I say, 'moved my stuff', it was basically a couple of binliners with my clothes in them. I didn't even own that posh pull-along suitcase that I arrived with! That belonged to the TV company.

Tiffany wasn't annoyed about me leaving. She said she felt sad I was going as she liked me, but she understood my decision. Tiffany is the only other person who knows about the money in my bank account. She says to me that I should go off and enjoy it.

'I don't think money does bring happiness, Shiraz,' she said to me this morning. 'But it brings you more freedom. Freedom to make your own choices. Like I've decided today I don't want big boobs any more, I want tiny little egg-cup sized ones like catwalk models have. I'm going to book myself in. It's going to cost a fortune, but what the hell, I've got the money to pay.'

I rolled my eyes and laughed when she told me that bit, 'cos I'm going to use my money for something much better than that.

The film crew were livid when I told them I was quitting. Well, for about ten minutes, then they wrote a storyline around it. They're going to say I couldn't handle the celebrity lifestyle and that I ran off in the middle of the night in a huff throwing my suitcase in the car in a mega tantrum. They've even got the footage to prove it.

'Whatever, bruv, jog on,' I said to Karen. Then I grabbed a lift with Maureen to catch the train home.

Life at Thundersley Road, Goodmayes, Essex hasn't changed much since I left. The house is still far too full of people.

My mother still don't trust all these 'foreigns' coming in the country down the Channel Tunnel.

Fin still has a sore ear and is throwing some mental tantrums.

Cava-Sue is considering running for local council as a Green Party member so she can nag an even larger portion of Essex to stop flushing their lavvies so often.

Clement is now officially barred by Nan from playing *Guitar Hero*.

My father is still doing everyone's heads in with his snoring.

Ritu still can't understand why everyone is so depressed all the time on *EastEnders*.

Murph and Lewis are still playing far too much Nintendo and it's driving Cava-Sue quite mental.

Penny still ain't slimline. In fact if anything, Penny is even bigger. Silly dog, I love the bones of it her, I do.

Oh, and I love Wesley Barrington Bains II. And Wesley Barrington Bains II loves me back and will do, forever. And that's why he'll understand when I tell him I'm finishing my A-Levels and going off to university to do a

BA Honours in English, won't he? I'm not telling him that now though. I'm not telling anyone.

I'm saving that adventure for later.

Can't get enough of Shiraz?
Then look out for the first of her slammin' diaries

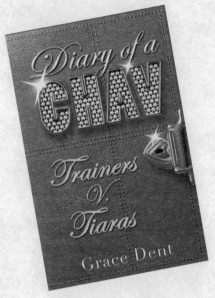

...TUESDAY – 8PM

Soapstars on Skates is on TV and our Staffy's snout is jammed up my armpit. Dad's got out the Karaoke machine, Mum's setting fire to the kitchen – least that's what it smells like – and Nan has dropped off on the couch. Yeah, BORED!

But hey, Nan's got me a buff leather diary for Christmas! So now, I – Shiraz Bailey Wood – can write down all my 'goings on': hanging round Burger King Car Park in Bezzie's Vauxhall Nova. Falling out with my hippy sister. Trying not to murder my little bruv. Definitely NOT thinking about school...
Keeping it real...

http://shirazbaileywood.bebo.com

Read on for a slammin' extract from
TRAINERS V. TIARAS

TUESDAY 25TH DECEMBER – CHRISTMAS DAY

So much for ramming the word iPod into every sentence since last June.

Nan got me a diary for Christmas! A pink leather one with a proper lock and everything. Nan reckons I should 'write down all my secret hopes and wishes' then hide it in a place where no one will ever find it. She never said why.

I would have asked why but she chucked me it, sank almost half a pint of coffee liqueur, then passed out snoring. She was making a noise like when Mum accidently hoovers our dog.

Well, it's Christmas Day and I've nothing else to do, so here goes . . .

THE SECRET HOPES AND DREAMS OF SHIRAZ BAILEY WOOD AGED 15

- I hope my boobs grow bigger soon and get proper pointy nipples.
- I hope my mum, Mrs Diane Wood, notices the boob growth and stops muttering to my dad, Mr Brian Wood, about taking me to get 'my bits checked out by Dr Gupta'.
- I hope I get a boyfriend this year as there is a running

joke amongst my sister, Cava-Sue Wood, and my brother, Murphy Wood, that I am a lezbitarian.

(Oh and Murphy, if you're reading this, BOG OFF you smelly turd. These are my <u>secret hopes</u>. AND I KNOW IT WAS YOU WHO WROTE 'SHIRAZ BAILEY WOOD FANGITA-EATER' ON THE FRONT OF MY GEOGRAPHY COURSEWORK.)

- I hope I can learn this year how to be nicer to lads in general. I wish I could be a good listener like my best friend, Carrie Draper. I wish I could learn how to flutter my eyelashes and remember funny lines from *Dog the Bounty Hunter* that make boys laugh. I wish I could stop giving boys dead arms and wedgies when they do stuff like fart near me.

- I hope by January, Mr Bamblebury, our headmaster, has forgotten about my part in the Mayflower Academy Winter Festival which resulted in a request for police presence.

- I hope the local newspaper, the *Ilford Bugle*, forgets that our school, Mayflower Academy (formerly known as Marlowe Comprehensive) came bottom of EVERY exam results and behaviour table in Essex. I really hope they stop calling us 'Superchav Academy' soon 'cos now everyone in Essex calls us it and it's totally embarrassing.

WE ARE NOT CHAVS, RIGHT?

OK, we're not ALL chavs. Me and Carrie AREN'T anyway. Uma Brunton-Fletcher down the road is a bit.

Can't get enough of Shiraz?
Then look out for the second of her
slammin' diaries

OH MY DAYS!

I've only gone and passed SEVEN GCSEs! Dad and
Cava-Sue are chuffed to bits. Murphy reckons I
cheated. Mum is pulling her best dog's bum face.
She's not happy, I can tell ...

So, Mayflower Sixth Form here I come! Time to ditch the
gold hoops and the spray tan and get myself a long
scarf, some A4 folders and a new pencil case.
Shiraz Bailey Wood is entering a new phase. Clever,
sophisticated and definitely not skiving off ...
Staying real ...

http://shirazbaileywood.bebo.com

I am the master of my own destiny.

Well, that's what Ms Bracket, my English teacher last year, always says.

'Shiraz Bailey Wood,' she says. 'The sky is the limit for a bright spark like you! You could be anything you want. Like an astronaut! Or a lion tamer! Or the Prime Minister! The only thing stopping you is yourself!'

She used to jar my head sometimes she did. She was proper obsessed about us passing our GCSEs. Ms Bracket isn't bothered about all that 'Superchav Academy' stuff. That's what a lot of snobby newspaper reporters used to call my old school Mayflower Academy, you see. And I'll say it again for the billionth time. . .

WE WEREN'T ALL CHAVS, RIGHT!?

(Jury's out on Uma Brunton-Fletcher, though.)

Ms Bracket isn't prejudiced and stigmatising towards young people like most grown-ups are. Saying that, she doesn't take any of our crap either. Like when I told her me and Carrie didn't need no English GCSEs 'cos we were starting a world famous singing duo called Half Rice/Half Chips.

'Fair enough, Shiraz,' Ms Bracket says. 'But in the

event that you *don't* become the next Beyoncé Knowles you'll need to get a job to feed and clothe yourself! SO DO YOUR COURSEWORK!'

In the end even I had to admit that passing my GCSEs was a better plan if I didn't want to end up flogging the *Big Issue* outside Netto. If you've ever seen that YouTube clip of me and Carrie on ITV2's *Million Dollar Talent Show* you'll know why. Oh my days, that was well shameful.

Ten pounds flaming ninety-two pence we spent on those matching red leg warmers and devil horns, then we only get one verse into 'Maneater' by Nelly Furtado and this snotty looking judge in trousers so tight you could see the outline of his trousersnake tells me I'm singing like someone strangling a donkey.

Yeah, BARE JOKES, bruv. Jog on.

Not like I cared though. I just laughed in his face. He was like thirty-three years old or something. A proper antique. It's not my fault if he couldn't appreciate me being an individual.

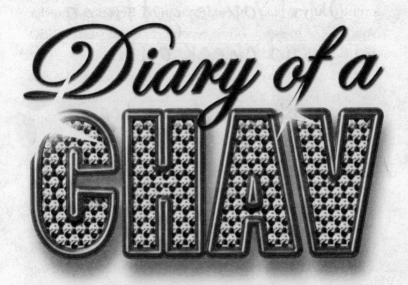

Keeping it Real

OUT NOW

OMG! You've gotta go and check out....

www.shirazbaileywood.co.uk

⭐ Read all about what's going on in Shiraz's world in her SLAMMIN' weekly blog

⭐ Join up to the TOTALLY MENTAL forum to meet and chat with other Shiraz fans

⭐ Exclusive BLINGIN' members' area for VIPs like yourself

⭐ Have your say and vote on what's hot and what's not, word of the week and much more... OH MY DAYZ!

Log on today at www.shirazbaileywood.co.uk
You'll be lovin' it – guaranteed!